"Is marryin[g]
you really [...]"

Anna's reply came quickly. "You have no right to ask, Andreas. None at all!"

"I have your interests at heart. We were brought up together, remember. In the ordinary way that should mean a lot."

"It means nothing, surely." Anna could not look at him for fear of revealing her true feelings. "I can't expect you to feel— responsible for me."

"It's not that. I just want to make sure you're not making a terrible mistake."

"By marrying someone who wants me— someone I could rely on, who would always be there when I need him?"

"That describes Nikos, but it would not be enough for the Anna I remember," Andreas replied evenly, yet his eyes betrayed a warning glitter.

"I've stopped remembering," Anna said, her heart too full of memories to answer truthfully.

"I'm sorry about that," Andreas said quietly. "I would have it otherwise."

Jean S. MacLeod, the author of more than fifty romance novels, lives with her husband on an isolated peninsula in Scotland's Western Highlands. From her doorstep she has a breathtaking view of the Hebrides. "In these surroundings," she says, "it must surely be possible to go on writing for a very long time." Indeed, her ideas and words are as fresh and romantic as ever.

Books by Jean S. MacLeod

The Apollo Man

Jean S. MacLeod

Harlequin Books

TORONTO • NEW YORK • LONDON
AMSTERDAM • PARIS • SYDNEY • HAMBURG
STOCKHOLM • ATHENS • TOKYO • MILAN

Original hardcover edition published in 1986
by Mills & Boon Limited

ISBN 0-373-02837-7

Harlequin Romance first edition May 1987

CHAPTER ONE

'ANNA!'

The girl sitting on the shore overlooking the tideless sea did not turn immediately, knowing that what she heard must be a voice from the past, thinking it strange that she should have remembered Andreas Phedonos so vividly as she sat there. It was six years now since he had gone, leaving the island with not one word of explanation after a final quarrel with her father. They had been so uncomfortably alike those two, quick-tempered and ready to take offence at times when none was meant, but it had been excusable in Andreas because he had been young and vulnerable at twenty years of age, with no parents of his own. Her father . . .

She sighed at the memory, looking out across the bay.

'Anna!'

She turned, struggling to her feet, her lips parted in a small gasp of incredulity. Andreas was standing there in the bright April sunshine; not the boy she remembered from six long years ago, but a grown man, resolute and determined, willing her to recognise him, tall and straight as an arrow as he had been in those far-off days, his head held high.

'You don't remember me?'

All the grief came flooding back, catching her by the throat. 'Nothing could be easier,' she told him. 'You are still the same.'

He smiled for the first time, shaking his head. 'I doubt that,' he said grimly. 'I'm six years older, for one thing, and a great deal wiser.'

'Where have you been?'

She hadn't meant to ask the question, telling herself that she didn't want to know. He had the look of a man of the world about him now, no longer the open-hearted boy she remembered so well.

'Here and there, learning to fight my own battles.'

'You could always do that,' she assured him, brushing the sand from her faded cotton skirt.

She saw him plainly now, darkly handsome in the strong light of morning, the blue eyes he had inherited from his English mother questioning her reluctance to welcome him, his level black brows drawn together in concentrated thought. How quickly he had changed from the Andreas she remembered to this self-assured and determined man!

'Your father is dead,' he said slowly, not questioning the fact. 'I heard that in Limassol. How did he die?'

'He was drowned on a fishing trip, coming back from Crete.' It was still difficult to talk about her father's untimely death.

'And Mama?'

The old term of endearment had slipped out naturally, she supposed, a confession of the affection he must still feel for the woman who had brought him up.

'She is well.'

He took a step towards her across the level sand. 'Is that all you have to say to me?' he demanded. 'Anna, I have come back to see your mother and try to make amends.'

She stiffened at his folly, forcing herself to remember the manner of his going. 'You can never do that,' she told him with a bitterness which surprised her. 'You hurt her too much.'

'I know. I said I was sorry.'

'Did you?' She faced him in the morning sunshine. 'I don't remember.'

He took her by the shoulders, looking down into her hostile eyes. 'I wrote a letter,' he said. 'It was never answered.'

'You're lying!' she accused him.

Releasing her, he turned to look back at the villa

standing on a terrace above the bay. 'I'm not trying to defend myself,' he said, 'but I did write. I owed it to her, you see, for all she had done for me.'

'She didn't expect gratitude. She won't now!'

'Is she here?'

'Yes, but I don't want you to go to her,' she said decisively. 'Not till I have seen her first.'

Her lips firmed in a determined line, protecting the woman who might even now be watching them from the house.

'To warn her or advise her?'

The abrupt question took her by surprise.

'To cushion the shock of your return,' she answered slowly. 'She has been ill.'

'I'm sorry. Is it serious?'

She looked at him steadily, remembering the disappointment of his going and all the grief it had caused. 'She has been advised not to work so hard.'

He looked away from the house to the long curve of the bay and the white hotels lining the shore. 'I was hoping to talk to you about that,' he said.

She turned then, grief and bitter memory blurring her vision. 'To make amends?' The words choked in her throat. 'You can never do that, Andreas, as long as you live!' She stood between him and the house. 'I can't stop you going up there,' she told him.

'No, you can't do that,' he said. 'I mean to go.'

His quiet determination infuriated her.

'It would be far better if you went away again without seeing her. You can only bring her sorrow—another parting.'

'That wasn't my intention.' The hardness in his eyes disconcerted her for a moment. 'I feel I have something to offer her.'

'I can't think what that might be.'

He studied her in silence for a moment.

'No, you couldn't, I suppose,' he said briefly. 'It is still all or nothing with you, Anna. I can see that.'

She caught her breath. 'You'll find her changed,' she warned. 'She has been very ill.'

'Is that a promise that I can see her?'

She hesitated. 'Give me time to explain to her.'

'Tell her the Prodigal has returned.'

'She loved you as a son!'

'I know that. Did you want me to forget?' he demanded.

'It didn't concern me!'

He caught her by the arm as she turned to go, looking steadily into her eyes. 'Didn't it, Anna?' he demanded. 'Can you honestly say it didn't matter to you at all?'

She forced herself to meet that relentless gaze. 'Not at all,' she lied. 'I only cared about my mother and what you did to her.'

'Going away without a word,' he suggested. 'Yes, that was unforgivable, but I think your mother would understand.'

'My father was always difficult,' she allowed. 'Quick to criticise, perhaps, but he had supported you. He wanted you to make something of your life—to take up a profession.' She looked at him again, seeing the distinction of his well-groomed appearance and the subtle air of authority about him which had been the first thing she had noticed. 'You have succeeded,' she said involuntarily. 'You have made something of your life, after all.'

'Not in the way he wanted.' His eyes sought the horizon. 'He could never see that I wasn't cut out for an academic career.'

Inwardly she smiled at the idea. 'No,' she agreed. 'But fundamentally he wanted the best for us both.'

'Have you found that sort of Utopia, Anna?' he asked. 'Have you married?'

She laughed at the question. 'I haven't had time for that. I have other things to think about,' she assured him.

'Such as?'

'Making a living. The home you deserted six years ago

is now a small hotel.'

He didn't appear to be surprised, looking at the villa on the slight elevation above the bay.

'It is an ideal situation,' he agreed. 'Are you doing well?'

She hesitated. 'Reasonably well. It is hard work, of course, but rewarding.'

'Hard work for your mother,' he said. 'Yes, I can appreciate that.'

'Don't pity her!' she cried. 'It's too late for that.' She walked a little way up the beach. 'I'll let you know if you can see her.'

His jaw firmed perceptibly. 'I haven't come as a supplicant,' he informed her coldly. 'I have a proposition to make.'

She looked back at him, her dark eyes accusing. 'Nothing you can suggest now can alter the past,' she declared. 'Nothing you can do.'

'Nothing is as final as that,' he said briefly. 'Where can I wait?'

She looked about her, taking in the neat breakwater they had built to make a small private harbour where a boat could be moored in safety when the Mediterranean surged in towards the land before a south-westerly gale, and up to the terraced gardens leading from the villa to the shore. Nowhere there, she thought, in full view of the windows.

'If you walk along the beach——'

He turned to face the sun. 'I know my way,' he said. 'I'll go as far as Candy's Place and then on to the road.'

'There's a public right-of-way now,' she told him. 'Candy had to grant the land.'

He nodded, striding off without looking at her again. She had made him angry, she thought, but anger was a very small thing compared with what he had done.

Slowly she walked up the beach on to the terraced gardens surrounding the villa where the scent of mimosa hung heavy on the morning air. Already the small golden

balls were falling from the trees, making a scented carpet
beneath her feet, their glory soon passed, but other trees
and shrubs were in riotous bloom, colouring the terraces
in white and blue and scarlet before she came at last to
the house.

Built of local white stone thirty years ago, the Villa
Severus faced the sea, its four ogival arches on the ground
floor providing a shady open veranda to counter the heat
of the noonday sun, its walls clad with yellow jasmine
and clematis in every shade from deepest purple to the
palest of pink. Above the Frankish arches long windows
lay open to the morning breeze, lace curtains stirring
fitfully as it passed, and over everything lay a peace and
tranquillity that could almost be felt. The ideal holiday
hideaway. It had been the only building on that part of
the coastline at one time until the encroaching hotels had
crept nearer and nearer to encompass it in the end. On
one side the massive tower block of the newest holiday
hotel looked down on the villa with scorn; on the other
Candy's Place hovered uncertainly on the shore-line
waiting to be taken over in its turn by the highest bidder
for its desirable frontage.

That would never happen to the Villa Severus, Anna
vowed determinedly. They would never sell out to a high-
rise block of concrete and a powerful name. Never!

The Villa Severus was full of memories for her,
although it had now been turned into a small hotel,
memories of her childhood and the happiness she had
known there, and memories of the time Andreas
Phedonos had come to stay there, adopted by her parents
because he was the son George Rossides had always
coveted and because her mother could never have
another child. Their parents had been lifelong friends
and the tragedy of Christine and Stelios Phedonos' death
had touched her mother deeply.

Andreas and Anna had grown up together at the Villa
Severus, sailing and fishing and swimming from the
beach or trekking into the mountains to climb hills which

seemed as high as the Alps in those far-off days, to come home exhausted to Dorothy Rossides' cooking and the prospect of the next halcyon day. Then Andreas had gone off to do his National Service and things had never been the same again.

She had reached the villa, halting at the terrace steps to collect her nostalgic thoughts. Everything was different now, too. Andreas was no longer a part of their family by his own deliberate choice and the loving home they had shared was now an hotel.

'Who was that you were talking to down on the beach?' her mother asked when she had walked the length of the terrace to find her standing on the loggia beside an open door. 'Was it Nikos? It looked like him.'

Her mother's eyesight had been dimmed by her recent illness, although she could see well enough to read her newspaper and the English books she loved.

'No, it wasn't Nikos.' Anna stood beside her, looking down towards the beach. 'Mama, I have to talk to you. Something unexpected has turned up.'

'About the hotel?' Dorothy turned anxious eyes in her direction. 'You have further word from the bank?'

Anna shifted her position, knowing that what she had to say must be said right away. Her mother had suffered many blows and much hardship since her father's death and some of the anguish was stamped on her face, but nothing had dimmed the beauty of her magnificent eyes. They were still a deep, luminous sapphire blue and still full of a tender understanding as she looked back at the daughter she loved.

'What is it, Anna?' she asked. 'You have bad news for me?'

'I hope not.' Anna glanced along the covered loggia to make sure they were alone. 'Mama, Andreas has turned up. He is back on the island—has been for several days, I gather—and he wants to see you.'

The silence which followed her announcement seemed to stretch into an eternity as Dorothy assimilated her astounding news.

'Don't see him if you don't want to,' Anna said at last. 'He doesn't deserve any consideration. Not when he went off like that without a word after all you had done for him—the love you gave him freely and the home Papa provided for him.'

'That was what we undertook to do,' her mother said quietly. 'When he was left alone in the world we provided a home for him, but we also gained the son your father wanted. It was a fair exchange, Anna. He owed us nothing.'

'Except loyalty and—obedience, perhaps.'

'Your father expected absolute obedience,' Dorothy Rossides agreed with a sigh. 'It was no way to handle a young boy of Andreas' nature. He had a strong will of his own. What is he like now?' Her eyes brightened. 'I can hardly wait to see him.'

'Mama, are you sure?' Anna was more than doubtful. 'It will bring back all the pain you suffered when he went away.'

'I can cope with that,' her mother said quietly. 'I know he will be changed, but at least he has come back.'

Anna moved towards the loggia door leading into the residents' lounge. 'There's something else you ought to know.'

Dorothy looked round at her questioningly, as if Andreas coming was all she needed to know.

'He looks—quite prosperous,' Anna said, 'and very determined. A man who might force his will upon you if you gave him half a chance, in fact. He also maintains that he wrote to you after he left and got no reply. I don't believe you wouldn't answer his letter so I told him he was lying.'

'Anna, how could you! You should have known him better than that.'

'I'm convinced I didn't know him at all!'

'He never told a lie,' Dorothy Rossides said. 'That was the thing I admired about him most. If he had done something wrong he admitted it and accepted the just punishment for his actions. You know that.'

'It was so long ago it can hardly matter now,' Anna said. 'You will find that he has changed in many ways if you want to see him,' she added.

'You wish me not to?' The clear blue eyes searched her face. 'Why, Anna? Why?'

'I think he has come back for reasons of his own, even though he says he just wants to make amends.'

'We can't be ungenerous,' her mother said. 'Where is he now?'

'Probably knocking on your front door.' Her tone was flippant to cover the annoyance she felt. 'He walked up through Candy's Place when I told him I had to see you first.'

'Why did you say that?' Dorothy asked. 'Because you thought we should harbour resentment for what happened so long ago?'

'I don't know.' Anna paused just inside the door. 'I thought he was over-confident, for one thing, and—decidedly autocratic. I thought he was sure about having his own way.'

'Confidence is often necessary when you are fighting your way in the world,' Dorothy reminded her. 'He needed self-assurance to do what he did.'

Anna turned. 'The letter he said he wrote to you,' she asked. 'Did you ever receive it?'

Her mother's eyes clouded at a memory. 'No,' she said. 'I never did, but it could have gone astray.'

'Letters don't go missing that easily,' Anna said. 'He never wrote it!'

'How can you be so sure? Anna, this isn't like you,' Dorothy chided. 'You have always been generous in your estimate of people—people like Nikos, for instance, who doesn't always tell the truth.'

'Nikos is different! He is loyal and—and caring and he has always been our friend,' Anna protested.

'And always will be, I hope.' Dorothy smoothed her

hair. 'Am I looking respectable?' she asked, dismissing further argument. 'Will Andreas see a difference in me, do you think?'

Anna put a protective arm about her thin shoulders. 'It isn't so long ago,' she said gently, 'and you haven't changed at all.'

At that hour of the morning they were alone in the sunny residents' lounge, some of their guests still at breakfast in the adjoining dining-room, the others in their respective rooms preparing to go out for the day to the various archaeological sites in other parts of the island or to spend the long, sun-filled hours relaxing on a sandy beach of their choice. There was so much to do on this magic island of her birth, Anna thought, and soon they would be able to accommodate their guests with a swimming-pool of their own out there on the terrace at the side of the house. It had been her ambition for a long time, but now she thought that they might just manage it for the opening of the summer season, if all went well. It was almost an essential of hotel life these days, although the sea was there, right on their doorstep.

'I've spoken to Nikos about the pool, by the way,' she said, 'and he thought it was an excellent idea. It wouldn't inconvenience us at all since it would have to be next to Candy's Place where there's plenty of room.'

'I can't see why people can't swim in the sea,' Dorothy said. 'You did, and Nikos and Andreas. There wasn't much talk of a swimming-pool then, or water-skiing or snorkelling, for that matter.'

'All the big hotels have these amenities,' Anna pointed out. 'I don't mean that we should have them for that reason. We could never hope to compete with the big hotels and I wouldn't want to. Mrs Calder-Bates told me yesterday that was why they came back to us so often— because we were a small, intimate concern and she felt as if she was coming home.'

Dorothy nodded. 'That's what we wanted in the first place,' she agreed, 'and I wouldn't like to see it vastly changed, but I suppose we do have to move with the times. Did Nikos advise you about the speed-boat?'

Anna flushed. 'He offered to pay for it.' She drew in a deep breath. 'Of course, I couldn't accept that, so he will hire out his own boat from the mole during the summer. One of the boys—Hannibal or Paris—will drive it when he can't be here himself.'

'I don't know what we would have done without Nikos,' Dorothy mused. 'He has treated us like his own family and he never left the island.'

'He had something to stay for,' Anna said slowly, 'with all those rich orchards and vineyards he will one day inherit, and acres of carob trees up in the mountains.'

'He works hard,' Dorothy reminded her, 'and he is unfailingly kind.'

Her eyes went beyond the open glass doors which separated the lounge from the entrance hall, searching for their unexpected visitor.

'He may have changed his mind,' Anna reflected. 'I didn't encourage him.'

'No! He's here!' Dorothy's pale cheeks were suddenly tinged with pink. 'He has not changed so very much.'

The man who had come in through the double doors paused for a moment at the reception desk as if he were taking stock of the changes they had made, and then he came steadily towards them, holding out both hands.

'Mama!' he said. 'It is good to see you, at last.'

Dorothy Rossides went quickly towards him. 'Andreas!'

He bent his dark head, kissing her on both cheeks.

'You have been ill,' he said. 'What have you been doing with yourself, working so hard?'

Dorothy shook her head. 'I am better now. Hard work, as you know, never killed anyone. I have a stupid heart, that is all. It lets me down at times,' she confessed.

'You look the same,' he said, appraising her openly. 'And the Villa Severus is the same, although it is now an hotel.'

'That was necessary when your—when Papa died,' Dorothy said, looking away from his questioning eyes. 'But we will not talk about that now that you are here. You will stay, of course, at least for a meal with us.'

He hesitated, looking across the stretch of parquet to where Anna still stood beside the lounge windows.

'Why not?' he agreed. 'We have much to talk about.'

Anna flushed scarlet. She had no intention of discussing the past, if that was what he was suggesting, and she was half-angry with her mother for asking him to share their meal.

'I'll get some coffee,' she offered. 'Would you like to take it on the loggia?'

She had pointed the question at her mother, determined to ignore him, but Andreas was not to be intimidated.

'Let me help you,' he volunteered. 'I can carry a tray.'

'There is no need,' she told him. 'Paris is still with us—and Hannibal.'

'Hanny must be a good age now,' he mused, following her to the kitchen in spite of her objection. 'Thirty, if he's a day.'

'Thirty-two,' Anna acknowledged. 'He and Paris are very loyal servants and we appreciate the fact.'

'You were lucky to have them when you needed them. How long is it since—your father died?'

'Five years. We had to make our decision about the house immediately and we wanted to keep it so—here we are!'

She had tried to sound matter-of-fact, although her voice had faltered a little as she remembered that moment of decision which had saved the villa as their home.

'It was the only way,' she said.

He followed her through the swing doors into the kitchen where two young girls were busy at the sinks, looking about him at the alterations they had made, the concessions to hotel catering which had been necessary to transform the homely old kitchen he remembered into an efficient unit for its present purpose.

'It must have cost you a lot,' he remarked with true Cypriot candour. Anna stiffened. 'In more ways than one,' she admitted, 'but it was what we had to do to survive.'

'I know how Mama must have felt.'

She faced him angrily. 'You couldn't have known!' she declared. 'Otherwise, you would never have left as you did or stayed away so long.'

'We're back to the letter again,' he said as the two maids left the kitchen. 'You refuse to believe that I tried.'

'We haven't any proof.'

He laughed a little harshly. 'Is that what you need, Anna? Absolute proof of everything?'

'I prefer to believe the facts. My mother never had your letter and no matter what it contained it could never have softened the blow of your desertion.' She filled the coffee jug, her hands shaking over the task. 'If you had explained before you went off as you did it might have helped as far as she was concerned.'

'But not with you?' He watched her automatic movements with the filter. 'I'm not here to apologise, as you said before. Only to offer help.'

She spun round to confront him face to face. 'And what does that mean?' she demanded. 'Perhaps you have come with the idea that you can buy your way back into our affections. Or is that too conceited a suggestion on my part?' She drew a deep breath. 'You evidently don't feel the need for forgiveness.'

He continued to look at her, faint surprise mirrored in his eyes. 'I have asked for it where I need it most,' he said blandly. 'Your mother is prepared to accept my return without rancour. Why can't you?'

'Because——' She watched the coffee filtering through the paper, unable to offer him any real explanation of the way she felt. 'Because it was a betrayal and I can't think of it as anything else.'

'If I had still been here when your father died I couldn't have done very much about it,' he pointed out reasonably enough. 'I was a liability to him before I left the island, a constant threat to his authority, and a heartache for Mama. I realised that later when I had managed to curb the temper I had inherited from my own father. We Cypriots are all alike, you know, one minute vivacious and full of the joy of living, the next confined to the depths, like Hades in the Underworld.'

'I never saw you "confined to the depths",' she told him.

'I have been, nevertheless, but at the age of twenty one recovers quickly. You see,' he added slowly, 'I had this overpowering desire to improve myself. Can you understand that or are you determined to be stubborn?'

'If you mean that you now have a great deal of money perhaps I should accept it as an improvement, but it certainly can't mean anything to us now. When we needed you most you weren't there.'

'I regret that, but I could hardly help it since I didn't hear about your father's death until recently.'

'And by then you were well on your way to the success you needed,' she suggested, laying out two cups and saucers on a tray. 'Andreas, you don't need to explain to us. I'm sure we understand.'

'At least, Mama does,' he decided, picking up the tray. 'You have only set out two cups. Does that mean you refuse to join us?'

She added a bowl of sugar and a cream jug to his burden.

'I haven't got the time,' she said. 'I generally drink mine in the kitchen.'

'Who does the cooking?' he asked, pausing at the swing door. 'Don't tell me you acomplish that, too.'

'We have an excellent chef who comes in from Limassol each day,' she told him remotely. 'You will sample his culinary expertise if you intend to stay for lunch.'

He took up her challenge immediately. 'That has already been settled,' he pointed out. 'I have your mother's invitation.'

'We serve it in the terrace room at one o'clock—early because some of our English guests like to have a long afternoon at their disposal to bask in the sun or go sightseeing. I don't think they can quite reconcile themselves to no twilight, you see, and everything getting dark around six o'clock.'

When he had gone, the doors whispering shut behind him, she stood by the table looking down at its immaculate white surface for a long time, watching the procession of the past filing before her eyes in heartrending detail, seeing the years between his abrupt departure from Cyprus and his return in all their cruel reality, the uncertainty and the worry and the final realisation that they would have to give up their beloved home. It had come as a shock to both her mother and herself that George Rossides had died practically penniless with nothing of value to leave them but the Villa Severus itself. That and the equivalent of a few thousand pounds, most of which had been used to settle his considerable debts, had been the full amount of their benefit, and they had to find a reasonable solution to the future. Her own future as well as her mother's, Anna realised, because she had never taken up a profession. Vaguely she had thought about teaching, but the blow had fallen before that day arrived. At fifteen she had been happy and carefree, like most of her school companions; at sixteen she had been faced with a decision which had concerned them both. Further education was out of the question as far as she was concerned, although it was many weeks before Dorothy Rossides would concede the fact.

'If only we had Andreas to advise us!' her mother had said more than once, but Andreas had gone, feathering his own nest in a foreign land.

The bleak thought persisted until Francis Previn pushed the swing doors ahead of him, making his customary entrance. Involuntarily she glanced at the clock, a suggestion which did not escape his watchful eye.

'How can I possibly arrive on time when the Market is in turmoil today, as every day! I stand for one whole hour waiting for a lost consignment of melons that nobody seemed to know about—or care!' he cried, shrugging his massive shoulders as he discarded his linen jacket to tie on an immaculate white apron. 'I must have those melons because they are on the menu for tonight and that is already printed!'

'I could put in a substitute,' Anna offered.

'No way!' Americans had also been among their clientele. 'I have now the melons and all is well. It is the time that I can not afford to lose.'

'I will send Elli Jacovides to help you,' she offered.

'Heaven forbid!' His dark eyes rolled upwards. 'I can cope. How do I not cope?' he challenged.

'You invariably do.' She had reached the swing door. 'I'm sure the lunch will be up to your usual standard, Francis.'

She heard him grunt as she walked away, wondering whether she should have offered her own help in the kitchen in such an emergency, but she had other things to do.

Taking a list from the office, she checked the bedrooms, making sure that towels and soap were replaced in the bathrooms and fresh fruit available in the little wicker baskets which graced every dressing table. There was also a complimentary bottle of the local wine to be found for the new arrivals, due in from Larnica that afternoon, and two wine glasses to be suitably polished. She went to find them, surprising her mother as she came out of the lift on the ground floor. Dorothy was alone.

'What happened to your visitor?' she asked. 'Has he taken cold feet and departed before lunch?'

Dorothy shook her head. 'Have you ever known Andreas to miss a meal?' she smiled. 'No, he is having a quiet look around on his own.'

'Assessing everything.'

'Anna, don't be so hard on him! It must be a nostalgic journey as far as he is concerned,' her mother suggested.

'Does he think we should have done things differently?'

'He realises that we had very little money to spend.'

'Mother! You haven't made him feel sorry for us?'

Dorothy shook her head. 'Not in the way you mean, but you know that Andreas always expected the truth, even as a boy.' She shifted the pile of towels she carried from one arm to the other. 'I was taking them up to the store,' she explained.

'Leave them and I'll do it when I go up with the wine,' Anna said. 'Why not put your feet up for half-an-hour?'

'I've been sitting down drinking coffee since eleven o'clock,' Dorothy pointed out, 'and listening to Andreas' ideas.'

'Ideas about what?' Anna turned sharply to look at her.

'About catering in general. He thinks the new swimming-pool is absolutely essential.'

'Two hours ago you were asking me why people couldn't be content with the sea!' Anna kissed her on the cheek. 'Mama, don't let him influence you with his charm. He has had six years to polish it, remember.'

'You're very hard on him.'

'I have to be practical. I learned that when we first came into this business, and so did you. We haven't much time for sentiment.'

Dorothy handed over the towels.

'I'll check the buffet,' she offered. 'Elli forgot to take the salad out of the crisper.'

She walked away across the stretch of newly polished parquet, small and distressingly frail-looking in her tight grey dress but with her head held high. There had been a new light in her eyes, however, when she had spoken about Andreas, and that could be dangerous, Anna thought, when he had no doubt come back out of curiosity and not affection. In her heart she had already accused him of that.

The wine and glasses delivered to the relative bedrooms, she glanced idly out of the window, admiring the view they had over the wide blue bay to the shimmering vista of Limassol where the trading boats came in. Today there was a white cruise ship waiting its turn to enter the harbour and several tankers queueing alongside. The island was growing more and more prosperous, she thought, and the harbour was already too small.

Beneath her on the sun-drenched terrace Paris was laying out extra loungers and adjusting the umbrellas to suit their guests while Hannibal was supervising the soft drinks at the beach bar. She could hear the automatic thud, thud of the liquidiser as he fed in the oranges and the clink of glass as the 'empties' were gathered into the wire baskets to be washed at the house. It was a never-ending task while the sun shone, and it shone most days even in April.

A speed-boat started up, breaking the silence as it towed a skier across the bay. It had come from the neighbouring beach where already a para-glider hovered under a red-and-yellow parachute before plunging into the sea. The new amenities, she thought, the almost essentials for a modern successful hotel. It was something they had always wanted to keep at bay, the high-rise concrete edificies which were so impersonal both outside and in. Of course, they made money for their impersonal owners who probably lived on the Greek mainland or even in Egypt. The one thing she had always appreciated was the fact that they were not overlooked because their original garden stretched on either side of them and her father had planted many trees. Certainly it was a prime site for an hotel; they had room to expand, but the only concession to growth they had made was to consider a swimming-pool at the end of the terrace. It was enough, she told herself, and the bank had agreed to advance them the money.

Fiercely independent, she was aware of the glow of satisfaction the transaction had brought, but it would be all the improvement they would be able to afford for a very long time. They would be in debt to the bank, but she could work harder to pay it off.

A figure moved at the end of the mole where their two boats were moored. Andreas! She watched him as he moved slowly towards the little stone 'lighthouse' he had helped to build so long ago. The trauma of his unexpected return made her catch her breath as he looked away from the sea to contemplate the villa and its environment in greater detail. What was he thinking? What was he planning to do?

Her heartbeats quickened. There was nothing he could do; nothing she wanted him to do now! Yet she continued to watch him with a scrutiny which was almost fascination. So far, he had told them very little about himself, but the suggestion of wealth was there, and power. Ruthlessness, too, in the way he had explained his long absence. 'I had this overpowering desire to improve myself,' he had said, challenging her to understand.

Well, he had been successful probably beyond his wildest dreams, but what did that prove?

She stepped out on to the stone balcony to adjust the chairs, placing the white wrought-iron table neatly between them as he moved back along the mole, and when she looked down to the garden again he was standing on the terrace beneath her.

'Have you time for a drink?' he asked.

A deep colour rose into her cheeks because she had hardly expected another confrontation quite so soon.

'I'm sorry! I have things to do,' she called down to him.

'What sort of things that can't possibly wait?' he demanded.

'Andreas,' she pointed out reasonably enough, 'I am trying to run an hotel!'

'Ah!' he said. 'Only "trying"?'

'You know what I mean.' She was angry with him now because he refused to take her seriously. 'The morning is our busiest time.'

He glanced at his watch. 'It is almost one o'clock. Your mother told me you'd be free by half-past twelve.'

'The chef was late coming in. I had extra work to do in the kitchen.'

'I saw him with your mother supervising the lay-out of the buffet. A mountain of a man who seemed to know his job,' he remarked.

'We were lucky to get Francis,' she said. 'He's a dedicated cook.'

'I never remember you being too fond of the kitchen,' he observed, his dark head tilted to look up at her.

'I had to learn.' She drew back from the balustrade. 'Quite often you have to do the things you don't particularly like in order to survive.'

He thought about that for a moment.

'How right you are,' he acknowledged at last. 'I think we have both changed a great deal in the past six years, Anna. Certainly I have.'

'Change isn't always for the best,' she said, 'but perhaps that hadn't occurred to you.'

Why was she being so bitter? He hadn't injured them in any way; just gone off when her mother might have needed him most, causing her unnecessary pain.

'I'll wait for you in the terrace room,' he called up to her.

Perhaps her mother would already be there, Anna thought, although she would never have thrust Dorothy between her and someone she—distrusted in the ordinary way. She was used to fighting her own battles.

Andreas was standing in front of one of the long windows overlooking the terrace when she finally stepped from the lift, her dress changed and her hair tidied to meet the afternoon.

'You look—refreshed,' he commented, 'and very

practical. What will you drink?'

'Nothing stronger than orange-juice, thank you. It is the best thing for quenching your thirst.'

He gave the order to Paris who was on duty behind the bar.

'That's what I missed most in England,' he said. 'Freshly squeezed orange juice with all the bits and pieces in it!'

'Yet, you chose to make your home there,' she challenged.

He found an empty table and waited for her to sit down. 'I had very little choice, Anna,' he said, 'and I didn't spend all the time in England. I travelled to France and Spain and America, learning my trade.'

She looked at him expectantly.

'I worked my way up fairly quickly,' he admitted, 'from commis to head waiter at first in one of the smaller chain of hotels before I decided to go in for management.'

She gazed at him incredulously. 'You're in the hotel business? I can't believe it.'

'Why not? It's lucrative enough when you do the thing properly,' he suggested.

'And you, of course, haven't missed a trick!'

Paris put their glasses on the table between them and he paid for their drinks before he answered her.

'I'm not going to ask you what makes you feel so bitter,' he said, 'because I think I know. I've waved the white flag as far as your mother is concerned, but I don't think there is any need for further surrender. I'm in a position to help you now if only you will accept my offer.'

She stiffened in her seat. 'We don't need help,' she assured him.

'You do, if you wish to expand,' he pointed out.

'We'll progress slowly,' she answered firmly. 'That's the way we have planned it.'

'Don't you think you are being rather short-sighted?' he suggested. 'It would be to your mother's advantage if you accepted help.'

He had pierced her Achilles tendon with the barbed arrow which could hurt her most.

'I try to make her rest,' she said, 'but she has such spirit. That is something you ought to know.'

'And much tenderness. It was what I remembered most in all these years between then and now.' He looked down at the contents of his glass. 'Anna, why are we sparring like this when we once agreed about almost everything?' he demanded. 'I thought I could come back to things as they were, not conflict like this.'

Her fingers closed around her ice-cold glass. 'Was that something else you set out to do deliberately?' she asked in a very small voice. 'Charm us back to accepting you as if the past had never been?'

He swallowed the remainder of his drink, appraising her with a distant smile. 'I see you will not be convinced,' he said. 'You are determined to consider the past six years unforgivable.'

'They were unforgivable! If only you had written from time to time—for my mother's sake' she added quickly.

'She has accepted the loss of my first letter,' he said quietly. 'She believes I was speaking the truth when I said I wrote offering an explanation. She has come to terms with it.'

'Which doesn't begin to compensate for all the heartache you caused!'

'No, that is true. I have already said I'm sorry.'

She turned to look at him. 'If you had stayed here,' she said, 'you could not have achieved so much success. That meant a great deal to you, I suppose—more than friendship and understanding.'

'It did mean a lot to me,' he admitted, 'but not more than understanding. I don't know whether I expected you to understand or not, but I had looked for friendship.'

'Surely that can't matter to you so much now that you have everything else.' She finished her orange juice as her mother came towards them. 'Shall we go in now before the rush begins?'

Dorothy greeted him with a smile. 'What do you think of our improvements?' she asked. 'I saw you out at the lighthouse.'

'I remember helping to build it,' he said, taking her arm. 'Nothing has really changed, although six years is a long time in one respect. I remember how you used to say that the years flew away without us noticing, and that is true. This morning could have been yesterday as far as I was concerned.' He waited in the doorway of the terrace room for Anna to catch up with them. 'This used to be your sitting-room,' he remembered.

'We've made changes,' Dorothy acknowledged wistfully. 'It is no longer a home.'

Oh, Mama, Anna thought, that's the first time you've expressed regret so openly!

A table had been reserved for them at a window overlooking the terrace.

'We're going to put the swimming-pool out there,' Dorothy told him. 'It's a natural declivity and very suitable, I understand.'

'It's where we found the Roman coins,' he mused. 'We were all very excited that day, wondering if we had stumbled on a fortune and vaguely disappointed when they had to be handed over to the authorities. Where are they now?'

'In the museum,' Anna said, 'where they rightly belong.'

He smiled as he made way for her at the buffet. 'What do you recommend?' he asked.

'You must choose for yourself,' she said. 'I don't know your tastes.' Not now, she thought. Not any more. 'Francis believes in one or two tried and accepted dishes rather than variety, especially at lunch time.' She helped herself to prawns and salad. 'If there is anything else you would like I can get it for you.'

He shook his head, approving the dishes set out before

them. 'Everything is fine,' he agreed, 'for a small hotel. Variety isn't really essential, although it is often expected.'

She watched him add some fat black olives to his plate, remembering how they had picked them from the trees as children, carrying them back to the house on the hill where they had spent their holidays away from the tiring heat of the plain.

'How long were you in England?' Dorothy asked as they sat down. 'Three years. I spent most of them in London and Cambridge getting the experience I needed. After that I went to America,' he explained. 'I suppose it was something of a revelation to me, altering the pace of life I had known for so long.'

'You made friends there, I dare say,' Dorothy suggested almost jealously. 'Good friends.'

'Only one,' he said, looking out over the garden. 'There wasn't time for more.'

'Was he in the hotel business?' Dorothy asked.

He smiled at her interest. 'She was Madam Hotel herself!'

'Oh!' Dorothy couldn't hide her surprise. 'A woman. Naturally, I thought——'

'Women can be business tycoons in their own right these days.' He laughed at her simple assumption that it must have been a man. 'Especially American women, though this one was Swedish. She was married to an American, however, and that was how we met.'

'Oh?'

Dorothy waited for him to enlarge on the confidence, but he changed the subject almost abruptly, enquiring about old friends in Limassol and Nicosia until the meal was at an end.

Half impatiently Anna pushed back her chair.

'The flowers will be in,' she explained. 'I have to arrange them while I have a moment to spare and my mother should rest for an hour.'

It was dismissal and he seemed to accept it.

'I'll see you again,' he promised, holding her mother's hands. 'I'm here for a week or two at the moment and I'm practically on your doorstep.'

'Where are you staying?' Dorothy asked eagerly.

For a fraction of a second he hesitated as he looked in Anna's direction. 'At the Crescent Beach,' he said. 'I find it very comfortable.'

It was the hotel next door. The four-star hotel next door!

Anna walked across the hall like someone in a dream, seeing her mother into the lift.

'Do you still play tennis?' Andreas asked. 'When you have time, that is.'

'Not too often.' She crossed to where the flowers had been delivered to Reception. 'I must see to these right away.'

'I thought you might use the Crescent courts,' he suggested. 'They're excellent.'

'And new and expensive,' she retorted. 'You'll enjoy playing there.'

'I would need a partner,' he said. 'That's why I asked.'

'I'm not on holiday,' she reminded him, picking up the flowers she had yet to arrange.

'Neither am I, but I expect to have some leisure time.'

She turned as she reached the office. 'Does that mean you are here on business?' She hadn't meant to be inquisitive or even faintly interested. 'Of course, it's no affair of mine.'

'It could be,' he said enigmatically, 'if you were prepared to listen to me, but you are not. Not at the present moment, anyway.'

And not ever, she thought defiantly. 'I must go,' she declared. 'I am wasting time.'

He put a hand out to stop her. 'Think about it, Anna,' he said.

'About playing tennis at the Crescent Beach?'

'About listening to what I have to say.'

'Why should I?' She met his eyes over the sheaf of

flowers, her cheeks as pink as the flush on the magnolia blossoms she held in her arms. 'I don't need advice, Andreas—especially from you.'

She saw his jaw tighten, knowing that she had stung him to anger.

'I think you'll ask for it one day, all the same,' he told her on his way to the door.

CHAPTER TWO

IT was three days before she saw him again. She was cutting mimosa from the garden trees when he came along the beach from the Crescent Hotel, dressed informally this time in light trousers and an open-necked shirt. It was very hot, and even the wind which blew up with unfailing regularity each afternoon at that time of year had failed to disturb the silvery eucalyptus leaves above her head.

'I've given you time to be less busy,' he pointed out. 'I want to talk to you.'

'I can't think what we have to discuss.'

A spray of the mimosa she had gathered fell at his feet and he picked it up before he answered her. 'Several things,' he said.

'If it's tennis——'

'No, it isn't tennis.' He fell into step beside her as she turned back towards the villa. 'I'd like you to come to Paphos with me to look at a flat.'

'Why me?' She could hardly believe that he had made such a personal request. 'Surely you are able to make that sort of decision for yourself.'

'I need a second opinion—a woman's opinion, if you like—and you know Paphos very well.'

Her mind flew back to the times they had spent there as children and, later, when they were growing up, to the memory of a dawning awareness that they were, after all, not brother and sister but two impressionable adolescents responding unconsciously to their romantic surroundings on this magic island where legendary Aphrodite, goddess of love and beauty, had come up from the sea.

'There must be someone else you can ask,' she suggested.

'Not at the moment.' They walked up the terrace steps. 'Everyone else is too busy.'

'It's a common complaint!'

'So I understand. But you will come?'

'No. Not today,' she amended for no very obvious reason.

'Then, tomorrow, perhaps?'

'I don't know. I never make promises I may not be able to keep.'

'We could take your mother.'

'No,' she said. 'That wouldn't be any sort of solution. She doesn't like motoring in the heat.'

'Tomorrow, then,' he said, not taking her refusal as a final answer.

'I can't promise. We're short of staff now that the season has begun in earnest.'

'I meant to ask you about that.' He stood between her and the glass door leading into the hall. 'Do you have a winter season yet—ski-ing and that sort of thing?'

'No. We would need a place in the mountains for that and it's a short-time luxury we can't afford.'

'It would add to your amenities,' he pointed out. 'Something extra for the winter months when the snow is there.' He looked at her keenly. 'Have you thought about it at all?'

She shook her head, wondering where their conversation was leading. 'It's much too grand an idea at present, having a second string to our small little bow, so why should I waste time thinking about it?'

'Because you are now a businesswoman.'

'Not like that. Not like your American friend.'

'Ah! Lara,' he said. 'No, you are not at all like her.'

She flushed at the implication, knowing her own limitations in that respect.

'Perhaps I shall learn, in time.'

'You will never be hard enough to be completely successful,' he predicted. 'I can see that in you, Anna, at least. You may be disappointed—even bitter—but not hard deep down at the core.'

'You imagine you know me very well!'

'We were brought up together,' he reminded her deliberately. 'We shared a great many things.'

'Except trust!'

He took the mimosa from her, following her across the hall.

'That's as may be,' he said. 'I hope I can prove you wrong.'

Her mother was in the small sitting-room overlooking the loggia and he went in to talk to her while Anna arranged the last of the mimosa in a blue porcelain bowl on the reception desk, adding a few pale mauve irises she had picked earlier in the sunken garden at the side of the house to give a more dramatic effect. She went to the kitchen after that and did not see Andreas leave.

'What did Andreas want?' she asked when she joined her mother for a belated lunch.

'Just to be friendly, I think.'

'And were you?'

'I hope I was polite,' Dorothy said. 'Anna, he is trying so hard to make amends.'

'By offering us help now that we don't really need it? You must see that he is trying to ease his conscience because he knows how wrong he was.'

'Your father pushed him too hard—in the wrong direction, I'm afraid.' Dorothy said, 'but that's all water under the bridge now and we can afford to be tolerant.'

'But not to accept him back into the family as if the past had never been!'

'Perhaps not.' Dorothy looked distressed, toying with her salad as if the heat had become too much for her. 'I think Helen Stylianu phoned, by the way. Paris took the message.'

'It will be about the tour,' Anna decided. 'Let's hope nothing has gone wrong.'

'Why don't you go with Helen tomorrow?' Dorothy asked. 'It would be a respite for you and we are never very busy on a Thursday.'

Anna hesitated. 'I might think about it,' she agreed.

It was a long time since she had been round the coast or up into the mountains; too long, she thought as she went in search of Paris to find out why Helen had phoned so unexpectedly.

'*Despinis* Stylianu will not come tomorrow,' Paris informed her gravely. 'She is unwell with her throat. It is impossible for her to speak at all.'

Which meant the tour would have to be cancelled, Anna decided, unless someone else would drive the mini-bus which they used to bring guests from the airport and to motor them round the island on sightseeing tours twice a week with Helen as their knowledgable guide. She realised that it would have to be someone who knew the history of the various archaeological sites they visited, someone with at least a part of Helen's skill. It would be no use sending Paris, who really only knew about the beach-bar and the hotel.

'I've decided to take the mini-bus myself,' she told her mother the following morning. 'We can't very well afford to disappoint twelve people who are terribly keen to go and who have already paid their fare.'

'You'll enjoy every minute of it,' Dorothy predicted. 'You can do it as well as Helen can.'

'I wouldn't say that,' Anna laughed. 'I've forgotten a lot of my classical mythology, for one thing, but I can certainly drive!'

Now that she had decided to take the mini-bus herself she saw it as an excuse to refuse Andreas' invitation to go with him to Paphos, a legitimate reason for turning down his request to walk back with him into the past, which would only prove traumatic and lead to further argument in the end.

When she phoned the Crescent Beach she was put through to him immediately. 'I'm sorry about the trip to Paphos, Andreas,' she began, 'but Helen Stylianu, our guide, is ill and I have to take her place on one of our tours. She is a most efficient guide and our guests look forward to the trips, so I can't afford to disappoint them. I'm sure you will understand.'

'Of course,' he said immediately if a little drily. 'Business before pleasure, Anna. You might have known I would understand, although you don't sound particularly deprived.'

'Deprived? Oh—of the pleasure of your company, you mean! Well, I hadn't thought of that, but I have apologised and perhaps you will find someone else to go to Paphos with you.'

'No doubt.' There was a lengthy pause, although the line remained open. 'Perhaps another time,' he said pleasantly before he rang off.

There was no point in feeling aggrieved, she assured herself as she replaced her own receiver. He had accepted her excuse and that was that!

The idea of going away for a whole day's motoring along the coast and into the mountains of the Troodos was certainly very pleasant, although she had acknowledged that her talents as a guide to the ancient temples of the gods and the vast areas of excavations which dotted the landscape could never match those of Helen Stylianu, who was a natural guide. She had no time to make notes, however, and she would just have to do the best she could and hope that people wouldn't ask too many difficult questions.

Deciding to arm herself with a bunch of reference leaflets, she was ready by half-past ten to pick up the small group which had gathered in the hall with cameras and extra film at the ready and woollen jackets in case it might be cold in the mountains. Mrs Walsh, a middle-aged divorcée, was dressed conspicuously in red 'because it came out well in the pictures against all that colourless stone', and the two Miss Crabtrees, from Cornwall, in England, were each armed with a heavy tome called *Footprints Among The Ruins*, which they would probably refer to along the way.

The others, Anna discovered, were vaguely interested in mosaics, so she turned the mini-bus in the direction of Limassol, hoping to interest them in the scenery along the way. She loved her ancient island home, glorying in its history and its roots planted firmly in the past, and she would do her best for everybody.

Mimosa and eucalyptus trees lined the bay and the Mediterranean sparkled in the brilliance of another perfect day.

'I've been so looking forward to this,' Mrs Walsh declared, sitting in the best seat beside her. 'I'm sure you will do just as well as the official guide, although it isn't your job.'

'I'll do my best,' Anna assured her, 'and we can always check on details. I think we ought to go straight to the castle first and another day you can concentrate on the town.'

'The castle will be just fine,' Mrs Walsh agreed. 'They always fascinate me with all their drama and history going right down into the past. We don't have anything like that in the States—well, not as far back, anyway, and I just loved being in England last fall when we went on a guided tour of castles. There were so many—and each had a different story to tell. Yes, it was sure fascinating!'

'We have a great many links with England,' Anna told her as she turned the mini-bus into the castle courtyard. 'This is where Richard the Lionheart married Berengaria of Navarre whom he crowned Queen of England on his return.'

'He must have been a very masterful man!' Mrs Walsh

decided. 'Making sure everyone obeyed him and winning battles everywhere he went. It was all so very long ago,' she mused, 'but things haven't changed all that much, with nations squabbling and fighting for no very good reason and powerful men getting their own way all the time.' She gazed up at the castle walls. 'Maybe Berengaria didn't want to marry him too much at first, but it doesn't seem to me that she had a lot of choice if he kept her here.'

The younger Miss Crabtree had been studying her book but she had also been listening to what was being said. 'She could have been in love with him, of course,' she pointed out. 'She came to the island as his fiancée, I understand.'

'Accompanied by his sister,' the elder Miss Crabtree agreed primly. 'She was Queen Joanna of Sicily, and Richard was on his way to Palestine on a Crusade.'

They piled back into the mini-bus and Anna drove out along the Paphos road, wondering suddenly if Andreas had found someone to go to Paphos with him to view the flat he wanted to buy.

Dramatically the Castle of Kolossi stood in the fields ahead of them. 'Does anyone want to go in?' she asked.

'Oh, yes, please!' It was almost a chorus of consent. 'What a view there must be from the top of the tower!'

She explained about the Knights Hospitallers and the Order of Saint John of Jerusalem as they filed across the drawbridge to the keep to admire the three vaulted rooms on the ground floor. Mrs Walsh pressed on ahead to inspect the kitchen with its large fireplace which 'you could get lost in if you were not careful'.

Both floors were lit by fine window-seats on to which the elderly members of the party sank with relief after negotiating the winding stairs, and Anna took this opportunity to warn them that the final stairway to the crenellated terrace above was both winding and, in places, dark.

'I should have brought a torch,' she confessed

belatedly, hoping that no one would fall.

Half the party stayed where they were, content with
the view they already had from the stone window-seats,
but Mrs Walsh puffed her way gallantly to the top.

'I made it!' she exclaimed, crossing to the high parapet
to look down over the fertile land beneath, to the Salt
Lake and the wide bay of Akrotiri glittering in the sun.
'They tell me these vine fields have been here for
hundreds and hundreds of years and the wine is still
exported to this day.'

'The Commandaria,' Anna said automatically. 'You
can order it at the hotel.'

She was not really listening to Mrs Walsh because a
man and a woman were standing on the far side of the
ramparts deep in conversation, so absorbed in what they
had to say to one another that they seemed oblivious to
anyone else.

Hastily she turned away. The man was Andreas. There
could be no doubting the fact as his tall figure seemed to
shut out the sunshine for a moment, his dark head bent
attentively, listening to what his companion was telling
him.

Someone asked her a question.

'Oh, yes—sugar. Sugar was produced here, too, in the
cane-growing villages,' she explained obligingly. 'You
can see the mill down there on the outside of the tower
and the aquaduct which carried the river water for
irrigation. Madder was also grown——'

She was aware of Andreas and his companion
standing on the edge of the small circle which had
formed around her, but she did not look up. He could
smile, if he pleased, at her inadequate explanations, but
she would not let him see that his unexpected presence in
the tower had shattered her calm.

Other questions were asked and she tried to answer
them, looking over the parapet to the vast plain below.
When she turned, Andreas and his companion were
standing in the archway ready to leave and he met her

eyes with a wry smile curving his mouth before he
disappeared down the winding stairway ahead of his
companion.

How arrestingly beautiful she was, Anna thought, but
it was no one she knew. Perhaps it was a fellow-guest he
had picked up at the Crescent Beach after she had
refused to go to Paphos with him, a woman who could
just as easily advise him about the flat he hoped to buy as
she could have done.

The image of the tall, elegant stranger stamped itself
on her mind: the pale, golden hair looped into a loose
chignon behind the shapely head, the classical profile
which seemed so much in keeping with her surroundings
that she might almost have lived in such a castle all her
life, and, above all, the blue, dark-lashed eyes which had
met her own for a fleeting moment as they passed,
smiling eyes which reflected the sunshine although a
shadow of remembered pain seemed to lurk in their
depths.

'And now for Kurion!' the elder Miss Crabtree
announced, looking at her map. 'We'll go there, won't
we?'

'Of course.' Anna seemed to rouse herself from a
dream. 'It's our next stop.'

She wondered if she would see Andreas and his
companion again, but no doubt they had gone straight on
by the main road to Paphos to view the flat.

Turning the mini-bus to the left, she drove up the
natural acropolis of the cliff which dominated the wide
arc of Episkopi Bay and the whole peninsula, with Cape
Gata splendid in the sunshine and the Salt Lake
glittering far below.

'Can we get out,' someone asked, 'even if it's only for
the view?'

Anna explained about the Mosaic of Achilles.

'Wasn't he the guy who dressed up as a woman,' a
cynical voice enquired, 'and then had a change of mind
when everyone else was going to war?'

'You'll see it all inside' Anna smiled. 'I'll give you a leaflet.' She intended to stay out in the sun, not because she might meet Andreas and his beautiful companion poring over the mosaics, she assured herself, but because the wind from the south blew strongly against her as she stood on the cliff, cooling her cheeks. This was the 'cool porticoes' of the ancients and she stood quite still, waiting for the time to pass.

When her small party rejoined her on the headland they walked to the theatre and the baths and then to the horseshoe of the stadium where she pointed out the starting-line for the runners and the seven rows of seats still visible among the stones. They had the vast amphitheatre to themselves; there was no one else to be seen.

Going back to the mini-bus, she drove them to the Sanctuary of Apollo Hylates through the grove of pines and cypress, and almost immediately she saw Andreas standing in front of one of the Doric columns. Etched against the backdrop of an incredibly blue sky, he seemed too engrossed in his companion to notice that they were about to be disturbed. Anna was alone. The others had gone off in different directions, marvelling at all they saw and pointing their cameras at everything in sight. When Andreas turned they were barely a few yards apart, but he did not seem surprised that she should be there. He held out his hand to the woman by his side to help her across the rough ground between them.

'I thought we would find you here,' he said to Anna, 'or at the White Rock, which is a must with most tourists.' He drew his companion forward, his hand gentle on her arm. 'Lara has fallen in love with our island,' he said, 'and she would like to meet you.'

Anna stood quite still, looking back into the flawless face of the other woman with a fascination which was difficult to explain. No immediate greeting came to her mind, no words which could possibly describe how she felt. It was as if they had met before, long ago when all

the ruined shrines and temples round about them had
been peopled by men and women of a different age and
culture whose emotions had been fundamentally the
same as their own. The older woman was holding out her
hand.

'Your wonderful, wonderful country!' she said in
accented English. 'I am much in love with it, and
Andreas has been so kind, showing me the places that
will interest me most. You also take strangers around,
Miss Rossides,' she added with a slow, enchanting smile.
'I heard you explaining to your guests about that
wonderful castle of Kolossi and I am fascinated by its
story. How well you explain everything that is past!'

The tone of voice, the interest in those compelling half-
sad eyes appeared genuine enough, yet Anna found
herself holding back from complete acceptance.

'It's part of my job, at least for today,' she explained.
'Normally we have a proper guide but she has a throat
infection and was unable to come.'

'Is that what happened to Helen Stylianu?' Andreas
asked. 'I wondered. By the way,' he added, 'this is Lara
Warrender. She has lived in America for a long time but
now she is considering Cyprus as a new home—a villa
somewhere in the mountains, perhaps.'

Anna waited for him to complete the introduction, but
apparently he had no need to do so. Lara Warrender
already knew who she was.

'I hope you will find what you want in the Troodos,'
she said almost stiltedly. 'There are plenty of holiday
homes there to chose from.'

Lara smiled. 'At the moment we are looking for a flat
for Andreas,' she said, 'but, of course, you will know
about that. He is determined to have a place which is his
own apart from the hotel.'

Andreas stood aside for them to walk along the narrow
pathway together, but Anna shook her head.

'I must wait for my party,' she pointed out. 'We are
going on to Pelea Paphos and the Temple of Aphrodite.'

'Don't forget *I Pètra toú Romioú*!' he laughed. 'It will bear retelling although it is only a legend, after all.'

Anna drew in a quick breath, aware that he was reminding her deliberately of the past.

'What is this legend that you keep so much to yourself?' Lara demanded, immediately interested.

'It's about a hero—a Greek—who was supposed to have thrown a large boulder from the top of the hill of Ktima at a false queen who had spurned his love,' Andreas explained without looking at Anna. 'It missed her, of course, and fell into the sea, where it can still be seen!'

'Perhaps we will go there, also,' Lara suggested, 'if it is on our way to Paphos.'

Andreas looked at his watch. 'I doubt if there will be time' he said 'if we are going on to Troodos after we have seen the flat. We can come back another day.'

Which meant that this was no casual friendship, Anna thought, as she turned back to collect her scattered party, no brief encounter in an hotel lounge which would last for a week or two and then be forgotten.

She drove away from the Temple of Apollo determined to dismiss Andreas and Lara Warrender from her mind for the rest of the day, but she could not avoid a stop at the legendary White Rock where Aphrodite, daughter of the foam and goddess of beauty and fertility rose out of the sea. So many times in the past she had come here, sometimes with Andreas and sometimes alone, and she was forced to remember him vividly as if he was by her side now, standing in that high place above the sea. She avoided a visit to the Rock of the Greek, however, telling her party that it was no more than an overdrawn legend which should now be entirely forgotten.

For the remainder of the tour she drove automatically, stopping at the places of greatest interest along the way, and eventually she made a detour from Pólis to a waterside taverna where they were served the fish of their choice from an enormous tank which the jovial proprietor whisked away to be cooked over a charcoal grill by his smiling wife.

'This is what I like!' Mrs Walsh declared, shedding her straw hat and enormous satchel on the table. 'Eating native! It isn't a bit of use going to the latest five-star hotel you can find and having a French menu thrust under your nose, no matter where you are.'

Anna advised them about the wine.

'You'll eat with us, of course,' Mrs Walsh insisted, 'and tell us all about that spectacular couple you met at—where was it, now? The Temple of something-or-other. I have it written down somewhere, but you know the place I mean. We saw you speaking to them while we were photographing the ruins.'

'He was a friend of my family at one time,' Anna told her briefly, selecting red mullet from the platter offered to her by the proprietor. 'It was—a long time ago.'

'He's so handsome!' Mrs Walsh sighed. 'And that elegant lady he was with? Don't tell me she is his wife. They were too-too perfect together!'

'They are not married,' Anna returned almost sharply. 'I don't know how long they have known each other. They could have met anywhere. In England even.'

'She's not English, by the look of her,' Hilary Walsh decided. 'Scandinavian, I would say—or even German. That fair, Nordic type isn't difficult to place.'

'Nationality doesn't come into it when she can look like that!' one of the younger men decided. 'She stopped me dead in my tracks when I saw her standing there among all these marble columns like some lost goddess looking for the way back to Olympus. And those eyes! Did you see them? Blue as the heavens above her, but dark too, as if life had dealt her a raw deal, one way or another.'

'Your imagination will land you in trouble one of these days,' his companion told him. 'Why don't you just order some wine and forget about Greek goddesses for a while—or even Scandinavian ones! I'm ravenous. I thought we were never going to eat!'

The taverna had been an excellent idea, Anna realised, as the lavish Cypriot meal was set before them and their choice of wine was poured by the proprietor himself who was determined to please everybody. There was no formality as platter after platter was placed before them and they ate heartily, looking out through the open windows to the sea.

When it was time to go they shook hands with their delighted host, promising to come again if they could.

The return journey through the olive and citrus groves evidently made their day complete, but for Anna the strong fragrance of orange blossom wafting towards them from the wayside orchards only served to renew old memories which she was trying so hard to forget. She had sought to put them behind her for ever, but Andreas' return and their meeting on those high cliffs above the sea had renewed them all, bringing back the long, warm summers of their youth to mock her brave resolve. Their friendship had been a very precious thing, strong yet delicate, and he had severed it deliberately when he had gone away.

The sun was setting when they finally reached the Villa Severus, the lights along the bay pricking out, one by one, to challenge the stars already appearing in the night sky. It was a relief to be home, but everyone seemed to have enjoyed themselves and she felt satisfied with the effort she had made to please them.

Mrs Walsh was first through the swing doors.

'We've got so much to tell your mother,' she declared. 'She really should have come with us.'

Anna had left the mini-bus outside for Paris to put away for the night and she hurried towards the office to make sure that nothing had gone wrong in her absence.

'Hullo, there!' a familiar voice greeted her. 'I thought you had gone to Paphos.'

'We did, but we were sightseeing, and that takes time!' She turned as a small, square figure came towards her with a tennis racquet under his arm. 'Have you been playing all afternoon, Nikos?' she asked. 'You look warm.'

'I've had time to cool off waiting for you for over an hour,' he answered reproachfully. 'I thought you would be back before five.'

She glanced at her watch as he followed her across the hall.

'We stayed longer than we should have done at Michael Parlou's taverna,' she admitted. 'He always makes you feel so welcome.'

'Why didn't you go to the hotel?' he queried. 'You would have been served more quickly there.'

'But not nearly so well, and I thought a bit of atmosphere wouldn't come amiss. Guests expect that sort of thing.'

'I suppose so. I heard about Helen Stylianu's sore throat. Did you have to go?'

'Of course. I couldn't very well disappoint everybody.'

He regarded her with a hint of impatience in his dark eyes. Nikos Masistas was a young man who had rarely been denied anything by his doting parents and Anna had always been a challenge to him. He had told her more than once that he adored her in his laughing, inconsequential way and she had never quite believed him, but she had found his attentions pleasing enough in some ways. He was a good companion, for one thing, amusing and undeniably kind, but she found it hard to take him seriously for very long.

'I came to ask you to dinner,' he said.

'Like that?' Her amused glance took in the shorts and white T-shirt he wore.

'I have a suit with me in my sports bag.'

He had taken her acceptance for granted, as he always did.

'I've been away all day,' she pointed out. 'I couldn't possibly go off again and leave everybody else to do my job.'

'We needn't go very far,' he protested. 'I had thought about the Crescent Beach.'

'That's next door,' she said. 'Even so, I'd still feel I was deserting ship. Ask me some other time, Nikos.'

He looked disgruntled, swinging his racquet idly as he considered what he had to say.

'I have some news for you,' he told her at last. 'Andreas Phedonos is back on the island.'

Anna put her handbag down on the reception desk.

'I know,' she said quietly. 'He came to call on us and I met him this morning on our way to Paphos.'

'You did?' He looked surprised. 'Why was he going to Paphos, do you think?'

'To buy a flat for himself. Evidently he wants a *pied-à-terre* on the island to come back to from time to time and perhaps to call home.'

'Which means he isn't going to live with you?'

'No!' Her response was sharper than she realised.

'You know that he is staying next door?'

'Of course!'

'With an attractive lady friend.'

Anna flushed. 'They are friends of long standing, I believe,' she said quickly. 'She was with him at Kourion this morning.'

'He introduced you?'

'Certainly. There was no reason why he should have kept his friendship with her under wraps, as far as I can see.'

'That's true. She's very beautiful, I believe, and older than he is, but that doesn't seem to matter very much these days. She's also extremely rich.'

'That could be possible.' Anna took up the afternoon mail which had arrived in her absence. 'Have you met Andreas?' she enquired, doing her best to remain indifferent.

'Not yet, but I'm looking forward to it.' He sounded less than enthusiastic. 'After all, we were part of the island at one time before we grew up and decided to go our own ways.'

'Yes.'

She wanted him to go, not wishing to discuss Andreas with anyone, especially Nikos.

'So, you won't have dinner with me,' he said. 'Not even here?'

'Here is different,' Anna smiled, 'if you can wait till nine o'clock. The dining-room should be almost empty by then when most of the people have had such a busy day.'

'I'll change and have a drink at the Crescent,' he decided. 'One thing about the tennis club you can come and go as you please. I may even have a swim,' he added, 'since their pools are floodlit.'

She was aware of all the facilities the Crescent Beach had to offer but not envious.

'It's a very well-run hotel, but it is not exactly what we had in mind when we opened the villa,' she pointed out. 'Once we have our own swimming-pool I'll be more than satisfied with what we have to offer.'

'You could let me help,' he said. 'It would be an investment as far as I'm concerned.'

She shook her head.

'No, Nikos, thanks all the same,' she said. 'I want to do this on my own. I've borrowed from the bank, but we'll soon be able to pay the money back. We had a good season last year,' she added with a certain amount of satisfaction, 'and I believe in ploughing our profits back into the business.'

'You talk like my father,' he laughed. 'Papa is always ploughing back something or other!'

'That could be why he remains so successful. How is he, by the way?' Anna asked. 'And your mother?'

'Thriving—both of them. They hope you will come to Stroumbi before long to visit them. They do not come to the coast very often these days,' he added, 'because there is much more to do in the mountains.'

'I don't blame them,' Anna agreed, 'especially with all

these spectacular valleys at their back door. I wish I had more time to enjoy them, but perhaps one day I will.'

'There's always the estate,' he assured her, 'although they will expect you to work.'

'It wouldn't be a hardship,' Anna smiled. 'The air is so wonderful up there, especially in the summer when we are gasping for breath down here on the coast.'

'You know the remedy,' he said, preparing to go. 'Marry me and come to the mountains permanently.'

'One day I may take you up on that!' she laughed. 'But not till I've paid for my swimming-pool!'

'You think of nothing but the hotel,' he grumbled. 'You're quite heartless, Anna, my love!'

'I don't mean to be.' She was more serious now. 'It's just that I want to do this thing properly for my mother's sake. She has been disappointed so often in the past, Nikos.'

'You know we would take care of her. She would be quite comfortable at Stroumbi as one of our family,' he pointed out.

It was the traditional Greek way of life, the commitment which the head of a family accepted to an older generation, making sure of their future together, and this time Anna knew that Nikos' offer was genuine. As the widowed mother of his young wife, Dorothy would be accepted with open arms at Stroumbi and cared for during the years she had left.

'I know you would be kind to her,' she said huskily, 'but this is her home. Being a small hotel hasn't made a lot of difference to her because she still has her own private rooms and can still potter around in her own beloved garden.'

'But she has to work, and so have you,' he protested. 'It can't be the same.'

'It's what we have accepted.' She put a warm hand on his arm. 'Don't try to disillusion me, Nikos, because we have a long way to go.'

'You are so determined!' He was half-exasperated by

her attitude. 'Perhaps you have something else in mind.'

She faced him squarely. 'If you mean *someone* else,' she said quietly, 'the answer is "no".'

'I was thinking about Andreas Phedonos,' he admitted honestly. 'He owes your mother a great deal. I thought perhaps he had returned to repay his debt.'

Anna flushed scarlet. 'There's no question of that,' she declared. 'There never could be. He caused her too much pain when he went away without a word.'

'He did his National Service with my cousin, Demetris Loizides, but after that they lost touch. Demetris said he was very ambitious, even at nineteen, and determined to succeed one way or another. He would learn a lot in England.'

'It seemed he travelled all over the world,' Anna said. 'He is quite different from the Andreas we knew and he has great charm. At least, my mother thinks so.'

'Does that mean she has totally forgiven him?' he demanded.

'I don't see how she could when she suffered so much at his hand,' Anna declared firmly.

'He argued so often with your father,' he reminded her. 'They could not see eye to eye.'

'That was part of his reason for going away. They were both very strong characters who had different points of view, one older than the other and, maybe, wiser.' Anna moved towards the sitting-room door. 'I don't know,' she said. 'It worried my mother very much because she loved them both.'

'He could have returned when your father died. Did he not know?' Nikos asked.

She shook her head. 'Perhaps not, and by that time he would be chasing his own particular rainbow.'

'Success,' he mused. 'He was always ambitious.'

It was a word Nikos hardly understood, nurtured as he was in the lap of luxury with a family fortune to depend upon and a large estate to call home.

'I must go,' she told him. 'I'll see you at dinner about

nine o'clock.'

Disconsolately he turned away. 'Why do you have to work such uncivilised hours?,' he grumbled. 'You should be fair to yourself and take time off—some time, anyway!'

'I've been pleasing myself all afternoon,' she laughed unsteadily. 'You know how much I like a visit to the past, and I never tire of looking at the mosaics.'

'Or meeting old friends on the way,' he suggested, not trying to hide his jealousy.

'If you mean Andreas, that was an accident,' she assured him, 'and he had his own lady friend with him. We only spoke for a minute or two and we really had nothing to say to each other.'

'I'll take your word for it!' He was his old, bright self again, swinging his racquet as he made for the door. 'See you at nine!'

Her mother was deep in conversation with Hilary Walsh and her daughter, who had not been on the bus tour because she had preferred to sunbathe on the beach all afternoon, acquiring an angry red colour which she hoped would develop into a flattering tan. She was a lumpy, fair-skinned adolescent who had very little to say for herself in company, outpaced and outshone by her mother who was the talkative kind. Yet, Dorothy seemed to enjoy their company, listening attentively as Mrs Walsh described their successful day.

Anna waved to them from the doorway and then made her way to reception where she checked the register and glanced through the mail. There were two letters requiring immediate attention and she had started to type her replies when there was a loud commotion at the desk.

'I demand to see the manager—at once, please!'

It was a woman's voice, loud and angry, someone obviously disgruntled by a fancied lack of attention, she thought, hurrying to the office door.

A red-faced, angry matron confronted her across the desk.

'Are you in charge?' she demanded. 'Actually, I want to see the manager.'

Evidently one of the guests who had arrived during the afternoon, it wasn't difficult for Anna to place her from long experience.

'If you can tell me what has gone wrong, Mrs Pope, I'll do my best to put it right,' she volunteered.

The angry lady looked her over with fine contempt.

'I still want to see the manager,' she insisted.

'I am the manageress,' Anna told her. 'My mother is the proprietress, but there is no need to disturb her. I'm sure I can deal with any complaint you wish to make.'

Mrs Pope, who was travelling with her sister, drew a deep breath.

'Shortly after our arrival some flowers were sent from a Limissol florist for my sister from an old friend of the family,' she announced. 'I rang from our room for a vase to put them in and, so far, nothing has happened. I have been waiting for over an hour.'

'I'm sorry!' Anna apologised. 'If you had rung down to reception I'm sure something would have been done. We have a change of staff at four o'clock and your vase could have been forgotten. I'm sorry!'

'Forgotten?' Mrs Pope could hardly believe her ears. 'It is your duty *not* to forget. These flowers will wither quickly in the heat of our room. I demand an explanation!'

Anna hesitated. 'I can only offer you an apology and accept the blame,' she said. 'I will find a vase for you immediately.' She came round the end of the desk, wishing that the irate lady would lower her voice because there were already several other guests in the hall. 'How many flowers do you have? I wasn't here when they arrived.'

'No,' Mrs Pope agreed, 'that's another thing. We did expect some personal reception, especially since it's such a small hotel, but apparently you were elsewhere or otherwise engaged.'

'We had an emergency this morning,' Anna explained patiently. 'Our guide on the mini-bus wasn't able to go on the tour we had arranged so I had to take her place.'

'I'm not concerned about that,' Mrs Pope told her, the angry colour still high in her cheeks. 'I'm pointing out that we take exception to being greeted by a beach employee of some sort in a pair of jeans and minus a shirt.'

Paris! Anna thought in alarm. Where had the others been?

'I do apologise.' She was genuinely sorry now. 'That sort of thing doesn't happen very often, I can assure you, Mrs Pope.'

'I should hope not! Quite apart from the indignity of the situation, it shows a marked lack of authority when guests are met in such a haphazard way by a half-naked beach-boy with imperfect English into the bargain.' Again the angry lady drew a deep breath. 'If that is an example of management I take a very poor view of it, I must say, and it won't be long before my sister and I find alternative accommodation.'

Anna kept her temper admirably. 'I'm sorry,' she repeated quietly.

'Apologising isn't good enough,' Mrs Pope declared, holding her ground. 'These flowers were delivered over an hour ago. Was it too much to ask for a vase as well?'

'It must have been an oversight.'

'Which is hardly my fault.' The strident voice rose to a crescendo. 'I am not responsible for your staff's tardy service. You are!'

Anna nodded in agreement. 'I'm sorry, but I can only apologise——'

'Leave this to me!'

Anna turned at the sound of his voice to find Andreas close behind her. He appeared to be neither angry nor exasperated by the tirade he had evidently overheard.

'Go and find a suitable vase,' he said under his breath, 'and send it up to her room.'

With a bland, placatory smile, he turned to Mrs Pope who appeared to be slightly disconcerted.

'That young woman has just told me she's the manageress,' Anna heard her complain as she rushed off obediently to find the missing vase.

When she came back from the store-room Andreas and Mrs Pope were smiling at each other.

'Mrs Pope would like some tea taken to her room,' he told Anna pleasantly. 'Her sister is a bad traveller and has been air-sick. I think we could find a remedy for that, too. Perhaps a rest before dinner and a little champagne would help.'

Stunned into unbelieving silence, Anna went to get the champagne, coming back with the bottle to find Andreas and her disgruntled guest discussing the relative merits of English hotels both in London and the provinces.

'We like Bath,' Mrs Pope was saying. 'It has an aura which pleases us, but this year we decided to do something different. We have always taken a keen interest in archaeology and my sister is anxious to see your mosaics, I understand they are justifiably famous and very well presented.'

'We take great pride in them,' Andreas agreed. 'Let us arrange a car to take you to Kourion.' He glanced sideways at Anna, as if reminding her of their recent meeting there. 'I can assure you it is well worth a visit.'

'How kind of you,' Mrs Pope acknowledged. 'You have gone out of your way to be helpful, Mr.——?'

'Andreas Phedonos,' he obliged with the slightest of bows.

'Ah—you are Greek!' Mrs Pope exclaimed. 'But surely you have been away from your native land for a long time.'

'Too long, I'm afraid,' Andreas said, glancing once more in Anna's direction, 'but perhaps I can remedy that one day.'

'By settling in Cyprus?' Mrs Pope enquired. 'It seems to be a beautiful island from what I could see from the car on our way from the airport.' She looked at Anna for the first time. 'That was one point in your favour,' she allowed. 'The car you sent to Larnaca to meet us was most comfortable, I must admit.'

Mellowed by Andreas' flattery, she even smiled.

'I must put this on ice for you.' Anna held up the bottle of champagne. 'Please accept it with our compliments.'

Crossing to the restaurant to find ice and a suitable bucket, she saw Andreas ushering Mrs Pope into the lift with the polished courtesy of the well-trained manager, something which distanced him even more from the tempestuous youth she had once known.

'Well?' he enquired when he discovered her crushing the bottle of champagne into ice. 'That went off all right, don't you think?'

'You charmed her completely.'

'Part of my training,' he acknowledged. 'It was rough going for you, I must admit.'

'I kept my temper!' she protested.

'Only just. I thought you were going to blow your top about the tardy service.' He took the bottle from her, settling it into the ice with expert skill and finding a napkin to lay over it. 'You were going white round the gills.'

'Mrs Pope was quite insulting without having much cause for it,' Anna said, 'but there was really no excuse for Paris. He knows he shouldn't wander into the house without a shirt, however hot it is outside! I really did agree about that, and I suppose I was also angry with Elli and Alice who should have been on duty by three o'clock.'

'It took me back a few years,' he smiled. 'You being angry, with that flush in your cheeks and the flash-point in your eyes. Fundamentally, Anna, you haven't changed. You are your father's daughter all right.'

She turned to face him. 'And that condemns me?' she

challenged.

'Not entirely. You have spirit, which doesn't always do in an hotel, but I can't imagine you without it. We have to bite on our tongues half the time to keep the peace, but it isn't always easy.'

'You do it very well,' she assured him, 'and "my father's daughter" isn't always in evidence. It was just—after a long day—I wasn't ready for unjust criticism. We do try our best here, but sometimes it isn't enough.'

He put a hand on her arm. 'Don't worry about it,' he said. 'It happens all the time, even in a five-star hotel. There are Mrs Popes everywhere, you know. I'll take this up to the dragon's lair and you can put your feet up for five minutes. You look the worse for wear.'

'Dishevelled, I suppose you mean?' Anna smoothed her hair. 'Well, I've been out all day doing a job I'm not trained for and making mistakes. I suppose you thought some of them amusing, especially at Kolossi.'

'On the contrary.' He lifted the ice bucket. 'I thought you were doing your best and there can be no harm in that. You brought the past to life very clearly. You really love this island, Anna, just as much as I do.'

'Yet you left it in a hurry,' she accused him, 'with no thought of the future.'

'There you are wrong,' he contradicted her solemnly, his blue eyes steady on hers. 'It was the future that took me away and it was what I worked for over the intervening years. I always intended to come back, whatever you may think to the contrary, but I wanted to return with something to show for those years. I've done that now and I mean to stay.'

Her heart pounded at the revelation.

'To marry here and settle down?' she asked sharply.

'That was the general idea.' His eyes glinted in the semi-darkness. 'Not the immediate goal, perhaps, but the eventual one.'

'Is that why you were looking for a flat at Paphos?'

'Part of the reason.' He had evidently no desire to

confide in her. 'At the moment it will be no more than a convenient *pied-à-terre*.'

'Did you find what you wanted?'

'We looked at two possibilities,' he said, following her to the door with the ice-bucket. 'One of them would have intrigued you, I think. While they were digging the foundations for the block they discovered the remains of an old acropolis and they have glassed in an ancient tomb. Quite empty, by the way. It had been pillaged centuries ago, I expect, but the authorities wanted to keep it intact. They didn't condemn the building—how could they when half our towns are built on the ruins of former civilisations?—but they wanted the tomb kept as it was because it was perfect in every respect.'

'So—what did they do, in the end?'

'Built round it. There was plenty of room so it sits there, behind glass, bang in the middle of the new flats and really it is quite a feature of the place.'

'It hasn't upset your plans—about the flat, I mean?'

'No. I think you would approve my choice.' He paused by the lift. 'Why don't you come out and see it for yourself?'

She held her breath. 'It wouldn't make the slightest difference whether I approved of it or not,' she said. 'I—I'm not at all concerned.'

'I thought you might be curious.'

'Curious? How could I be? You have your own life to lead and I have mine. Whether you buy a flat at Paphos or not can't possibly be my concern.'

Deliberately he pressed the button to summon the lift.

'It was at one time,' he said. 'We shared most things—remember?' The lift doors opened and closed behind him and she was left staring at them with a foolish sense of disappointment in her heart. But why should she care what sort of flat he had bought at Paphos or anywhere else?

She found her mother in the small sitting-room recovering from Mrs Walsh.

'I've heard every detail of your busy day,' Dorothy smiled. 'How that woman can talk! I don't think she missed one single thing.'

'It's just as well she wrote most of it down in her diary,' Anna laughed, 'and I gave her plenty of leaflets to take home with her.'

'She was most impressed,' Dorothy said, 'especially with Andreas. She calls him the Apollo Man!'

'It's the sort of thing she would say.'

'Was he on his own?'

Anna hesitated. 'No. He had a very beautiful lady with him. Probably Mrs Walsh thought of her as the Aphrodite Woman!'

'Was she so very beautiful?'

'Yes. Andreas introduced her as Lara Warrender.'

'It's an English-sounding name—the Warrender part, anyway.'

'I think she is Swedish—Scandinavian, anyway. There was the hint of an accent, although her English was very good. She may have lived in England for some time.'

'Did Andreas meet her there?'

'Mama! I don't know. He didn't say where they had met or how long ago.' Anna crossed to the open door leading on to the loggia. 'Now, suppose you tell me what *you* have been doing all day. Were there any problems?'

'None at all! I rested, as you said, after lunch and Paris brought me some tea at four o'clock.' Dorothy smiled at her. 'I'm leading a much too peaceful existence nowadays, thanks to you, my dear,' she acknowledged. 'You carry all the burdens.'

Anna continued to look across the garden to the sea. 'One of which is a terrible woman called Mrs Pope who was demanding her pound of flesh and an ounce or two over for good measure.' she said.

'Oh, dear! Did she upset you? Paris said she had arrived this afternoon demanding everyone's attention and was displeased with him.'

'No wonder!' Anna turned back into the room. 'I must

have a word with Paris. He was wandering about without a shirt when Mrs Pope arrived.'

'He had one on when he brought my tea,' Dorothy excused her faithful retainer. 'We couldn't do without him, Anna. You know that. He is so very, very loyal.'

'That's what makes reprimanding him so difficult,' Anna allowed, 'but if we are going to run an hotel—even a small one like this—we must make concessions to people like Mrs Pope and her sister. None of the boys wander about without a shirt over at the Crescent even when they are on beach duty.'

'They have a sort of uniform,' Dorothy mused. 'Blue linen trousers and a white T-shirt with a blue crescent on it. All very smart, I must say. Everything matches their blue-and-white motif, even their beach umbrellas and the awnings on the tennis pavillion.'

'Which reminds me that I've asked Nikos to dinner,' Anna remembered. 'He was playing tennis at the Crescent Beach and wanted me to have dinner with him, so I invited him to come here instead. I've reserved a table for nine o'clock.'

'You should have gone with him to the Crescent,' Dorothy said. 'You might have picked up a few hints.'

'We're not running that sort of hotel, Mama, although sometimes I wish we were,' Anna admitted. 'Everything seems to run so smoothly over there. Nothing ever seems to go wrong, like forgetting a flower vase or being short of melons when they are already on the menu. It would be a saving on champagne at least!'

'On champagne?'

'I've just had to send a placatory bottle up to room twenty-three.' Anna hesitated before the questioning look in her mother's eyes. 'Andreas suggested it— pouring oil on troubled waters, or champagne, if you like. He came in while Mrs Pope was haranguing me on our shortcomings. Her sister had some flowers sent and there was no vase to put them in.'

Dorothy turned round in her chair. 'Andreas?' she

asked. 'What was he doing here?'

'Now that you ask, I'm not very sure. He arrived in the middle of the scene and charmed Mrs Pope out of her mind with the utmost aplomb. He has certainly developed the art of pleasing in a big way since he left the island, but I'm sure you must have noticed.'

'I have seen a difference in him,' Dorothy agreed. 'He's more mature and—I suppose "polished" is the word I want. Where is he now?'

'Coming down in the lift with a vast smile of satisfaction on his face, I dare say.' Anna moved towards the door. 'Do you want to see him, or shall I make your excuses for you?'

'We can't be rude,' Dorothy decided. 'This was once his home.'

'But not any more.' A dark colour rose into Anna's cheeks. 'If he hurts you again, Mama——'

'He won't do that,' Dorothy assured her with conviction. 'It is all over now and he has expressed his sorrow.'

'Hiding behind letters which perhaps were never sent at all!'

Dorothy looked beyond her to the restless sea. 'We have to accept his word,' she said. 'Letters can go astray.'

Before Anna had time to answer Andreas was at the door.

'Don't run away,' he said when she attempted to pass him. 'I want to talk to you. I want to talk to you both,' he added, taking Dorothy's hands in his. 'Have you half-an-hour to spare?'

The look in her mother's eyes made Anna hesitate. Dorothy was asking her to agree to his request. She sat down on the chair nearest the door, waiting for him to speak.

'I'm wondering if you would like to sell some of your land,' he said directly. 'A strip on either side. You have more than you need for such a small hotel and it's all sea frontage with good sand. It would be easy to extend the breakwater to make a longer harbour for more boats, and

I already have the lease of Candy's Place.'

Anna gasped. 'You mean—you've bought it?'

'I'm hoping to. It's entirely wasted as it is. Candy hasn't done a thing to it in twenty years. He's a beachcomber and always will be. He'll move off elsewhere—farther along the coast, I expect—and start again selling pop and sandwiches when he isn't fishing. He feels that the large hotels are encroaching on his privacy now and he doesn't like it.'

'And what do *you* intend to build on Candy's land?' Anna asked coldly. 'Another big hotel?'

'Not at the moment.'

'And you would like some of our land to enlarge it when you do decide to build,' she suggested.

'More or less. I'm prepared to offer you a very good price for it and I think you would be foolish not to agree. All that scrub area at the side could be landscaped to your own advantage as well as mine.'

'And we would be nicely sandwiched between two high-rise hotels with very little land to call our own.' Anna rose to her feet. 'No, thank you, Andreas. We don't need to sell our land, and if we did——'

'It wouldn't be to me?' His dark eyebrows shot up. 'Maybe I deserved that, but I really do mean what I say. In any case, the money for your land would not be mine. It would come from the syndicate who already own the Crescent Beach and I can guarantee that all they want to do is to enlarge their small harbour area and build terrace gardens down to the sea.'

Dorothy said, 'It wouldn't be like building on to the Crescent Beach,' as if she was pleading his cause.

'That could be the next step,' Anna pointed out. 'Mama! we don't need the money, whatever argument Andreas has to put forward.'

'It would pay for your swimming-pool and keep us out of debt to the bank,' her mother suggested.

'We have already arranged all that.' Anna's cheeks were flushed, her eyes defiant. 'It's all we want for the present and the bank overdraft won't be a problem. I've thought it all out very carefully, Mama, and we don't need further advice.'

'Oh, dear!' Dorothy looked distressed. 'I wish we didn't have so many problems, especially when I am such a burden to you, not pulling my weight.'

'When you become a burden I'll let you know,' Anna said, deliberately avoiding Andreas' eyes. 'In the meantime we're managing nicely without any outside help and that's the way I like it.' She moved towards the door. 'Nikos will be here early, I expect.'

Andreas followed her into the hall. 'Nikos Masistas,' he remembered. 'Is he still as persistent as ever?'

'He's still the same person I've always known,' Anna said. 'He hasn't changed at all. He did his obligatory service in the army and then came back to work for his father.'

'A well-planned future, I must admit. I met a cousin of his on Samnos, but that was a long time ago. He hasn't married?'

'No.'

Andreas smiled. 'That surprises me. He has nothing to wait for.'

"Except the right girl to marry!'

He turned back towards the sitting-room. 'I think he always knew who that was,' he said. 'Why haven't you married him, Anna? It can't be because he hasn't asked you.'

The distressing colour of confusion rose in her cheeks again. 'I'm not ready to marry anyone,' she said sharply. 'Not yet.'

'The day will come,' he predicted maddeningly. 'Dare I say that I hope I'll be here to see it?'

'You can say anything you like,' she answered, 'but just don't go back in there and upset my mother. She won't sell anything to you against my better judgment, Andreas. You can take my word for that.'

'I wouldn't dream of distressing her,' he said more

seriously. 'I respect her too much for that.'

'All this talk of selling the villa upsets her. You ought to know how fond she always was of her home,' she said.

'I didn't ask her to sell the villa,' he pointed out reasonably enough. 'All I mentioned was a small strip of land on either side of you which isn't so very important to you, anyway.'

'It gives us privacy!' She turned to face him. 'If we sold it to your syndicate they could build right up to our terrace wall. It may be scrub land, but it keeps the villa the way it has always been—a private place a little bit apart. Some people want that sort of holiday, you know.'

He looked down into her angry eyes. 'One day you may change your mind,' he said. 'When you do I hope you will come and tell me. I mean to develop Candy's Place,' he added thoughtfully, 'but not in the way you imagine. I'll clean it up a bit and alter the frontage, but I don't think you need fear another high-rise hotel on that side. I'll keep the eucalyptus trees and a strong wooden fence between us.'

'You would have to honour the right-of-way from the road to the beach,' she informed him.

'I've gone into all that with Candy. He feels we have struck a good bargain and it was more money than he had expected.' He paused at the terrace door. 'I've half a notion he was ready to go, anyway. The fishing isn't so good these days.'

'I can't imagine Candy's place without him.' Her tone was unconsciously wistful. 'He was always there. I remember how he taught us to fish from that awful boat of his and what fun we had when he found the old outboard that wouldn't start till he kicked it.'

'I thought you might have forgotten all that,' he said, 'but I'm glad you haven't.'

She drew back instinctively. 'I have other memories, too,' she said, 'and they aren't all so hilarious as Candy's outboard. I'm glad you're not going to spoil his place, Andreas, but that's all I can say. I don't suppose you'll be

staying there permanently, anyway, when you have
found a flat in Paphos more to your liking.'

'Candy's will run itself with a good manager in,' he
said. 'It's just something I wanted to do. Call it a whim, if
you like, but I've always liked the sound of Candy's Place
and I think the bay needs a bit of atmosphere. There are
enough four-star hotels as it is. I won't go in to see your
mother again,' he added. 'There will be plenty of time for
that later.'

He left her with a brief smile and after a minute or two
she saw him going down through the gardens to the
beach, making his plans for the future, no doubt.

CHAPTER THREE

NIKOS MASISTAS, neatly dressed and scrubbed clean,
arrived at the villa at exactly a quarter to nine, crossing to
the reception desk where Anna was handing over to Elli.
He looked at his watch, comparing it with the wall clock
above her head.

'Dead on time!' he remarked. 'You can't still be
working?'

'I'm almost ready. Elli will take over till midnight.'
Anna closed the register she had been studying. 'My
mother is in the sitting-room,' she added.

'I came to see you.' He was determined to wait until
she was ready to go with him. 'We haven't talked for
ages.'

'Almost three hours!' she teased. 'It isn't exactly a
lifetime.'

'I meant seriously,' he insisted. 'I know we talk all the
time—about nothing—but honestly I think we should get
down to discussing the future.' The telephone rang in the
office and Elli went to answer it. 'Anna, it's time we
made a bargain. Even if you won't marry me right now at

least we could be engaged.'

Anna glanced across the hall. 'What a place to make a proposal!' she said.

'There you are! I said you wouldn't talk seriously and you have proved me right,' he grumbled.

'Nikos,' she said gently, 'I don't want to talk about that now. When I promise to marry you I want to be quite sure.'

'We've known each other long enough,' he pointed out. 'We've always got along well. Why are you so reluctant to see things my way?'

'Because—marriage can be such a lottery,' she told him solemnly. 'So many things can go wrong.'

'Not if you are in love.'

'Even then. Besides, I've got so much else to consider,' she decided.

'Your mother and the villa,' he suggested. 'But I've already promised your mother would be taken care of at Stroumbi and you could sell this place for quite a profit.'

She shook her head, the possibility stabbing at something in her heart. 'I could never sell her home over her head while she wanted it.'

'But it is already an hotel!' he protested. 'It's already changed, Anna. You can't get away from the fact.'

'Perhaps not, but she can still sit out in her beloved garden in a certain amount of privacy and she can still look at the sea,' She drew in a deep breath. 'That's the way I would like to keep it.'

'She could visit the coast whenever she liked,' he insisted. 'We're not a stone's throw from Pólis or even Paphos, for that matter. She could even have her own flat there.'

'It wouldn't be the same, and I can't imagine my mother in a flat. She is too fond of her garden and a window-box just wouldn't do.' Anna moved round the end of the desk. 'Can we talk about this some other time, Nikos? Already she will be wondering where we are.'

'I'm going to keep talking about it till you agree,' he

informed her stubbornly. 'I want to marry you and
something may happen to make you change your mind.'
There was a sense of urgency in his pleasant voice which
had never been there before. 'I've waited a long time,
Anna, and you could never have been in doubt about my
faithfulness.'

'No,' she said gently, 'I never have. You haven't
changed at all, Nikos, and I'm sorry if I've hurt you,
but—but I just can't promise you anything now. So much
has happened in the past few days——'

'Such as?'

'I—we've made a lot of decisions about the villa and
the immediate future,' she pointed out. 'I—couldn't
burden you with our debt.'

'Is that all?' He guided her towards the bar. 'I wish I
could think there was nothing else to worry about but
what you owe the bank to pay for your new swimming-
pool. It would be the easiest thing in the world for me to
wipe the slate clean.'

'I know,' she agreed, 'but I can't accept that sort of
gesture, Nikos. It would be the reverse of a dowry,
wouldn't it, taking something instead of bringing
something to the marriage, as I should?'

'Dowries are things of the past now.' Scornfully he
swept her argument aside. 'It's a worn out idea these days
and my family has no need for one. I have quite enough
for us both, and even if you didn't want to live at
Stroumbi I could make a home for you elsewhere.'

They had reached the open doorway to the bar and
suddenly she saw Andreas sitting there at a table
overlooking the loggia. He was not alone. Sitting beside
him in the flattering light from one of the overhead
lanterns was his companion of the morning, the
'Aphrodite Woman' as she had named her lightly when
Mrs Walsh had called Andreas the Apollo Man. They
were looking around them, as if appraising the quiet
atmosphere of the Villa Severus, and no doubt Andreas
was wondering why she had refused to sell her surplus

land when such a generous offer had been made for it.

Anna drew in a sharp breath. Her mother was nowhere to be seen and already Andreas was on his feet, making way for them at the loggia table.

'We came over for a coffee and a drink,' he explained. 'Lara likes a walk beside the sea before bedtime.'

Lara Warrender smiled up at them from the sofa she was occupying. 'You have great peace here,' she said, 'and I appreciate that. Are you able to join us?' She moved a little way along the sofa, making room for Anna to sit beside her. 'We dined early because of Martha who exhausts herself during the day swimming and playing tennis.'

'Martha is Lara's daughter,' Andreas explained. 'So far, we haven't been able to convince her that archaeology is quite interesting on site. Hence her reason for staying behind at the hotel when we went to Paphos this morning.'

Stunned by the knowledge that his fascinating companion had a daughter old enough to play tennis on her own initiative, Anna turned to introduce Nikos, but the two men had already acknowledged each other.

'You two haven't met,' Andreas said to Lara. 'This is Nikos Masistas, a loyal Cypriot who never left the island after he did his National Service. Nikos, meet Lara Warrender, a very good friend of mine.'

The two shook hands while Anna looked round for her mother.

'We're going in to dinner at nine o'clock,' she explained. 'Perhaps Mother is checking on our table.'

'I saw her going up in the lift ten minutes ago,' Andreas offered. 'Will you sit down?'

'Let me buy you a drink,' Nikos suggested, settling himself opposite Lara as if he was liable to stay there for the rest of the evening. 'What will you have?'

'Nothing more, thank you,' she declined. 'We only came in for a short rest before going back along the beach. I find an evening walk beside the ocean the very best thing for sending me to sleep immediately when I go to bed.' She turned to Anna. 'I was absolutely fascinated by your descriptions at Kolossi,' she said. 'You must love your island almost as much as Andreas does. He never tires of talking about it and I think he is glad to be home, at last.' She looked at Andreas quite tenderly. 'However far you travel there is always one place calling you back,' she added, 'and for Andreas it is Cyprus. There can be no mistake about that. When we decided to come here he was delighted.'

She knew so much about Andreas in her quiet way, Anna thought, speaking as if she had known him for a very long time. How long, she wondered, and how well?

'You've been around a bit, I suppose,' Nikos was saying to his old schoolfriend, adding with typical Cypriot candour, 'it looks as if you have found success in your life.'

'Reasonably so.' Andreas appeared to be amused.

'You left very suddenly,' Nikos reminded him.

'That's true.' Andreas glanced across the table at Anna. 'We won't discuss it now, Nikos, if you please.'

'Why not,' Nikos demanded almost truculently, 'if you have nothing to hide? Nothing you're ashamed of.'

Anna waited, aghast, for Andreas' reply.

'We are often ashamed of what we do in the heat of the moment or after an argument,' he said evenly, 'but it's foolish to let it colour our lives for ever if we can't do anything about it afterwards. When we've said we're sorry that should be enough.'

'Not always,' Nikos argued, suspicious of the way the conversation was going. 'Some things might be beyond forgiveness.'

'We can always hope not.' Andreas rose to his feet, holding out his hand to Lara. 'Time to go, I think. It's a fair way back along the beach and you haven't a coat.'

He was taking great care of her, Anna thought, wrapping her in a warm blanket of concern which spoke of love.

'I'd like to have met your mother,' Lara said. 'Andreas has spoken so frequently about her, but you will want to go in to dinner as soon as she arrives. Perhaps we could meet, though, some other time?' The blue eyes with their half-sad expression lingered on Andreas' face. 'At the Crescent Beach, perhaps,' she suggested. 'We will be there for another two weeks till Andreas gets his flat.'

A wave of ice-cold water seemed to wash over Anna before she could reply. 'I think my mother would like that,' she agreed truthfully. 'She is quite pleased to have company when I am so busy here.'

'Then, it is settled!' Lara smiled at her. 'Whenever it is suitable for your mother to come you will phone me?' She took Andreas' proffered arm. 'Good night, Anna,' she said deliberately. 'I know you will allow me to call you that.'

'She's absolutely ravishing!' Nikos declared as she walked away. 'Do you think there's anything between them? Sexually, I mean. You heard what she said about the flat.'

'Yes, I heard.' Anna's voice sounded harsh, even in her own ears. 'But—it isn't our business, is it, Nikos? They are both old enough to do what they like with their lives.'

He looked across the table at her with hurt, enquiring eyes. 'What is Andreas to you?' he asked.

'Nothing.'

'You mean that?'

'Why would I say it if I didn't?'

'I wonder if he's come back to stay,' he said jealously.

'I don't think so.'

'He may fancy himself back here at the villa managing everything for you,' he suggested tentatively.

'I'm sure that won't happen.' Her voice was determined. 'We don't need his help. When we did he wasn't there.'

'Which means you're not inclined to fall on his neck and kiss him or even to kill the fatted calf in honour of his return?'

'Something like that,' she agreed, 'though I can't quite see Andreas as the Prodigal Son.'

'He's come back for a reason, I think,' Nikos said. 'A reason of his own which has something to do with Lara Warrender. Do you think Mr. Warrender is vastly wealthy? Or she might be his equally wealthy widow, if Andreas plans to marry her.'

'We don't know that!' Anna exclaimed. 'There's no point in being dramatic about their relationship when we don't know the truth. She's—lovely and desirable, I grant you, but she may not even be free to marry anyone.'

'Hmm. Maybe you're right,' he said as her mother came to meet them.

It was several days before Anna saw Lara Warrender again. Some of their guests had departed by the weekend and there was what her mother called 'a lull' in the activity of the villa until the middle of the week when two more would fly in from Germany to be met at Larnaca by Paris with the mini-bus. It was a time to relax a little, but also a time to plan for the immediate future. By June summer would be upon them in earnest with its hosts of visitors and there would be more need for a swimming-pool than ever so their hope was that the new pool would be almost ready for the influx of holidaymakers. Already the contract had been signed and the work was scheduled to go ahead steadily during the slack period between. Because the pool was to be built well to one side of the villa itself, there had not been any need to close even while the excavations were in progress and a canvas shield had been erected between the terrace and the shrubbery which was now in the process of being cleared.

Anna hated to see even those trees go as she walked down to the beach for a breath of sea air before it was time to prepare the buffet lunch everyone seemed to enjoy. They were shabby old friends, carobs and ragged eucalyptus and overgrown hibiscus offering only a few jaded blossoms at the best of times, but 'the jungle', as they had called it, had been part of her youth, part of the happier rememberings which she had always kept in her heart.

How far away those days seemed now, she thought; gone into the mists of time! If nothing had happened to her peaceful life, if her father hadn't died and Andreas hadn't gone away——

She pulled up her thoughts there. 'If only' was a phrase she had never intended to use and self-pity was something she despised. Her life was now set in other ways and she turned her face to the future. With the scrub land cleared and the pool tiled and ready for use something else would be achieved.

She looked along the curve of the bay to where the blue-and-white sun-umbrellas of the Crescent Beach appeared beyond the dividing wall, thinking how ship-shape everything was over there. Their harbour was full of pleasure boats, children's pedallos and speedboats and, farther out in the bay itself, the white-hulled caique which made day trips to the larger bays in the west and along the northern shoreline. It was all so lavish and sophisticated and well-adjusted, with never a thing out of place, and beach-boys springing into action as soon as a guest appeared to find a suitable sun-bed for them under a natural tree or to adjust an umbrella to the right angle against the sun.

Well, she hadn't wanted that, and certainly they would never achieve such perfection, but there was no reason to bring it nearer by selling some of the precious land between. It was her protection, she thought; the privacy they advertised.

Her eyes swept round their own tiny bay, along the curve of the sand and out towards the miniature lighthouse which Andreas had helped to build so long ago. He had gone out there along the mole the other day, standing to look back at the villa, and now someone else was standing there, a child in a pink sun-dress with a straw hat on her head who seemed to be revelling in her isolation on the very edge of the harbour wall. She seemed too young to be out there alone and Anna moved quickly down the beach towards her.

Crossing the sand, she looked around for someone who might be with their unexpected visitor, but only her own guests were settled on the sun-loungers achieving a desired tan or reading undisturbed under the umbrellas which she had bought recently to adorn the beach.

When she approached the miniature lighthouse the girl had turned her back, gazing down at the waves as they lapped gently against the breakwater. She was older than she had looked from the terrace—perhaps six or seven years of age—and there was something almost forlorn about the droop of her shoulders as she contemplated the sea.

'It's very calm today,' Anna observed conversationally, 'even out there beyond the breakwater.'

The child turned immediately, studying her with large, sombre eyes. 'I like it when it makes waves against the rocks,' she said. 'Are you someone from the little hotel?'

Anna nodded, hoping that her visitor would move back from the very edge of the mole. 'I'm Anna Rossides,' she introduced herself. 'I live there and the hotel belongs to my mother. It was once our home.'

'I like it better than the Crescent Beach,' her visitor told her. 'It is more like a house and it has a real garden. I like it here very much.' She turned back to the miniature lighthouse. 'It isn't a real lighthouse, is it?' she asked. 'Not like the big ones along the coast. Was it one you made?'

Anna hesitated. 'It was built when we finished the breakwater—by someone I used to know,' she explained. 'We needed a light out here when it was dark in the winter and—he thought it would be in keeping with everything else. We built it together——'

'Do you have to light it every night?'

'No. We switch it on from the house. It's most convenient.'

The dark eyes continued to search her face, eyes that

seemed curiously familiar all of a sudden.

'I'm not supposed to be here,' her visitor announced, 'but I didn't want to play tennis any more. The coach is very strict and I'm expected to learn quickly, but I would rather swim when it's so hot.'

'George is a very good coach. He is very patient,' Anna said.

'And I am too impatient. Mama is always saying so.'

'You need to have patience to learn,' Anna pointed out, 'and it's lots of fun.'

'Do you play tennis at the Crescent Beach?' was the next question.

'Not very often,' Anna had to admit. 'I was once a member of the club but I gave it up.'

'Would you like to live in a big hotel—all the time, I mean?' The dark eyes were fiercely penetrating. 'I hate it! Everybody wants to know who you are and what you are doing when they don't really care.'

Amazed at such insight, Anna wondered if her small visitor might be older than she seemed. 'I think they care, in a sort of a way,' she said, 'otherwise they wouldn't stop to ask. They may be interested in little girls and how they spend their time.'

'I'd like to spend all my time swimming.'

'You have two lovely pools over at the Crescent Beach,' Anna reminded her, 'and soon we will have one here, too,' she added for the sake of conversation. 'We are going to build one up there on the terrace at the side of the house. They are preparing it now, cutting down the trees, which I don't very much like,' she confessed.

'I saw some trees yesterday with oranges on them. They were in a field—hundreds and hundreds of trees— and we were allowed to pick some oranges. Have you got an orange tree?'

'Sadly, no! We have to buy them in the market along with the other fruit.' Anna sat down on the top of the wall. 'You're English, I think,' she suggested.

'I'm American,' her visitor corrected her, 'but we used

to be English. We went away from England after I was born.'

'Oh, I see.' Anna looked along the beach to where a hurrying figure had appeared from the far side of the dividing wall. 'I think someone is coming in search of you.'

'Oh, that will be Susan,' her visitor said. 'She is always looking for me for something or other.'

Anna smiled, holding out her hand. 'Shall we walk down to meet her?'

'If you like.' There was a certain amount of reluctance in the childish voice; a desire to stay where she was. 'Maybe it's time for lunch.'

'Almost,' Anna agreed. 'You can come back again, if you like, so long as you don't go too near the edge and fall off on to the rocks.'

The child took her hand. 'Do you know,' she said confidentially, 'she follows me everywhere.'

'Susan, do you mean?'

'Yes. She's paid to look after me when my mother is away. My mother is a very busy woman.'

The final statement sounded like a repetition of a fact she had often heard, but Susan was hurrying towards them now, so Anna didn't question it.

'Can I really come back here?' the child asked urgently. 'Just whenever I like?'

'If you bring Susan with you next time,' Anna agreed. 'If she's supposed to be looking after you she will feel anxious if you just walk away.'

'She was talking to one of the beach-boys at the bar. She takes such a long time to finish her orange-juice!'

A breathless Susan came running along the mole. 'You know, of course, that you are trespassing,' she said sternly. 'You were told to keep on your own side of the wall.'

'I know.' The child gave Anna an appealing look. 'But I can come here if I want to now, and so can you. We've been invited,' she added importantly.

Susan looked questioningly at Anna. She was a small, pert girl in her early twenties with short, cropped hair and inquisitive eyes which seemed to sum up the situation immediately.

'You must be Miss Rossides,' she said. 'I've heard about you. You're very lucky to have a house like this so near the sea.'

'I think so.' Anna turned to move back along the mole. 'It really is all right for you to come over here,' she added. 'The beach is quite free.'

'We shouldn't need any more space than we have at the Crescent.' Susan was studying her carefully. 'They have everything one could possibly want over there, don't you think?'

'Undoubtedly,' Anna agreed. 'It's that sort of hotel.'

'I'm loving it!' Susan declared. 'Especially the beach. Everything is so relaxing, but when one feels energetic there's lots to do into the bargain. I'm dreading the end of it all.'

'How long are you here for?' They had reached the end of the mole.

Susan shrugged. 'A week—two weeks, I don't really know. It could be as long as a month.'

She took the child's hand 'Come on, Martha! Time to go!'

Martha? Anna stood looking after the two retreating figures for over a minute before she turned away. Martha! This must be Lara's child.

It seemed quite obvious now—the name, the pensive eyes which had stirred a chord in her memory as soon as they had met. Martha's eyes were dark, but they had the same look in them, as if the child had been brought up very close to tragedy and often felt neglected. With Susan to look after her, of course, she was safe enough, but it seemed that Lara had little time for her daughter.

Angrily she hurried back to the villa, telling herself that it was no affair of hers, but Andreas was Lara's long-time friend and surely he could have put in a word for a forlorn child?

She supervised the buffet lunch, helping to clear away because most of the kitchen staff went off for an hour at three o'clock, returning to the sitting-room to find her mother blissfully asleep in a chair with the morning pape clasped to her chest. There would be work to do in reception, letters to write and bills to sort out, and everybody else would be asleep in their respective rooms or sunning themselves drowsily beneath the sheltering umbrellas on the beach. It was the time of day when she was most often alone and able to take stock.

Sorting out the letters which had arrived with the morning mail, she noticed that the main contractors were about to start on the swimming-pool, moving in to work on the foundations the following morning, which was good. They were quick workers, doing a good job, and she could now count on the pool being ready for the summer rush.

The doors opened, letting a little rush of welcome air into the hall, and she glanced up to see who their visitor might be. Lara Warrender in a white linen suit and matching hat stood uncertainly on the threshold for a moment before she came towards the desk.

'I hope I'm not interrupting,' she said with a quick glance at the scattered papers. 'I came to apologise.'

'For Martha?' Anna guessed. 'You don't have to. She was charming.'

'We warned her about trespassing, but I suppose she just didn't think. Children never do when they see something which intrigues them.' The enchanting smile was genuinely warm. 'It was the little lighthouse that took her fancy, and Andreas was able to explain about it over lunch. She knew that he had helped to build it, so I expect you told her.'

'Yes.' Anna cast about in the turmoil of her thoughts for something else to say. 'It was an idea we had, supervised by my father.'

'The news of his death shocked Andreas,' Lara said

thoughtfully. 'I think he didn't expect it.'

'It was sudden. He was drowned five years ago while he was out fishing,' Anna explained. 'That's why we turned the villa into an hotel—to pay our way.'

She wondered why she should be offering such personal details to a complete stranger who probably knew all about her already.

'It isn't always easy, is it?' Lara said. 'Coping with something unexpected like that, but the need to work can be a blessing in disguise in some ways. I've worked very hard myself over the past few years, trying to hold a business together, and I think I've succeeded. What I would have done without Andreas, however, I don't know. He's been a tower of strength to me in so many ways.'

'I'm sure you've helped him, too.' Anna's voice was noticeably cold. 'He's achieved a great deal since he deserted the island, which was what he wanted, I'm sure.'

The vividly blue eyes searched hers. 'Sometimes it's necessary to leave a beloved place to gain the experience we need,' she said. 'Andreas could not have stayed in Cyprus and satisfied his ambition. I recognised that as soon as we met, and I needed someone to help me over a bad patch. I'm in the hotel business, as you must know, and I could see how eager he was to make good. He was star quality and I needed that sort of dedication at the time. He has proved extremely loyal.'

Anna tried to deny the fact, but could not. Andreas had obviously been loyal to this beautiful, wealthy woman he now served.

'I'm sorry you feel that you could not let us have some of your surplus land.' The businesswoman in Lara was evidently hard to suppress. 'We would have extended judiciously, but it was your choice, of course. I think Andreas felt that you didn't want to be overshadowed by our great height, but that could have been discussed. The original plan was to build more tennis courts and perhaps another pavilion, which you could have shared. We're a consortium, but we don't build indiscriminatively.'

'I—we're fundamentally opposed,' Anna smiled. 'The small hotel feeling its way and the de-luxe giant not having to care very much about future prosperity.'

'Oh, but we do!' Lara protested. 'Before we expand we have to think very carefully, weighing up the odds for and against. I think that is what Andreas and I find so stimulating,' she added. 'Expanding can be something of a lottery, however it is done, and we both like a challenge. Soon he will be appointed to the Board and I think that will satisfy him.'

Anna looked down at the scattered papers on her desk. 'I have a lot to do,' she said. 'Can I order you some tea?'

Lara shook her head, taking the hint. 'I mustn't delay you, but I would be very glad if you would come over to the Crescent Beach for dinner with us one evening. It would please Martha,' she added quietly. 'She has spoken much about you.'

'I have already refused Andreas,' Anna said. 'You know how busy one can be, even in a small hotel.'

'This would be for Martha,' Lara said deliberately. 'You were very kind to her.'

'For Martha, then,' Anna agreed, wondering why she should have given in to this woman who seemed to have everything.

'Will you bring your mother?' Lara asked. 'I feel that we will have much in common.'

It had been so quickly settled, Anna thought, rising to walk to the door with her unexpected visitor, but then Lara Warrender was no doubt used to getting her own way when she really put her mind to it. Backed by her position as a member of a powerful consortium and by her obvious wealth, there was probably nothing she couldn't do, no personal wish she could not easily fulfil.

'Shall we say the day after tomorrow?' she asked when they had reached the door. 'Andreas will be in Athens all day tomorrow and I'm sure he will wish to be there.'

Anna nodded. 'Do you wish me to come early?' she

asked. 'We dine very late, as a rule, but you said that Martha——'

'She would never forgive me if we sent her to bed before you arrived,' Lara declared. 'Do you mind very much coming early?'

'No, not at all.'

'Would seven o'clock be all right? It would mean nine before she was in bed, but it could be counted a special occasion,' Lara smiled. 'She loves to stay up late. Andreas would indulge her if he got half a chance, so I have to put my foot down most of the time. I'm the Ogre while Andreas plays the Knight in Shining Armour, you see!'

With a brief wave of her hand she walked away, the smile still on her lips and some of the sadness gone from her eyes.

The following day was a busy one, the sort of day that Anna had come to expect towards the end of the week. She did the bulk marketing herself, going into Limassol early to park her car as near the market square as possible so that she could bring some of the softer fruit back with her. It was while she was inspecting some fish on her way out that she was aware of being watched from across the street, but the stalls were so crowded with early shoppers that it was difficult to pick out anyone in particular. The sensation of being watched, however, persisted, but it wasn't until she had reached the junction of Hellas and Gladstone Streets that she recognised the diminutive figure of Susan hurrying to catch her up.

'Hullo, there! I wondered if I would be able to attract your attention,' she said breathlessly. 'I saw you coming out of the market but I was on the other side of the road and there was so much traffic and people milling around I just got across in time to miss you!'

Anna looked round for Martha.

'She isn't with me,' Susan informed her. 'It's my morning off and she's having a lesson from the tennis coach before it gets too hot to play. Her mother will be in the hotel all day so I thought I would seize the opportunity to buy a pair of shoes. But where to go? Every second shop seems to sell shoes.'

'I can tell you where to go,' Anna agreed 'depending on what you are looking for.'

'Oh, something smart with a highish heel. I'm small, you see, and I feel demoralised in flatties except on the beach.' She paused. 'I say, you wouldn't come with me, would you? I know you must be busy, shopping and all that, but I would appreciate your advice. Then perhaps we could have a coffee or something before we went back to the daily grind.'

'I mustn't be too long,' Anna said, 'but I'll come with you if you like. There's a very good shop quite near here—quite reasonable, too.'

'Oh, don't worry about the price,' Susan said airily. 'I get frequent presents from my employer because I do her duty for her rather well.'

Anna led the way across the street in silence.

'Pity I don't take her size in shoes,' Susan chattered on. 'I do very well with dresses, though, because I can shorten them to suit me. She buys the most expensive clothes, mostly in Paris and New York.'

'Do you go to America with her?' Anna found herself asking.

'Not very often,' Susan said. 'She goes home then and takes Martha with her, but I've half a notion she plans to stay here for a while. It would be easy enough for her to hop on a jet at Larnaca and be in London or Paris or even New York in next to no time. The thing is—she would expect me to stay here, too, and I don't know that I would want to do that. I like to travel. That's really why I took the job in the first place and I'm not sure that a villa in the mountains would be my cup of tea.'

She paused for breath and Anna seized the opportunity to change the subject.

'We can go in here and see what they have to offer,' she suggested, indicating the open door of the nearest shoe shop. 'I think you'll get what you want.'

'Oh, yes, thank you!' Susan dived into the shop ahead of her. 'Can you translate for me?'

'You're quite safe with your English,' Anna assured her. 'You don't really need me to come in with you.'

'But please do, all the same! I like to have a second opinion.'

It was almost an hour before they emerged, leaving the floor strewn with rejected shoes, but Susan had made a decision in the end and the assistant saw them off the premises with a pleasant smile.

'Let's have that coffee,' Susan suggested. 'We've still got time. Can we go somewhere with lots of atmosphere, not just to a fashionable coffee-shop?'

'There's one round the next corner,' Anna said, 'but I must be on my way home by eleven o'clock. Some of the things I've bought will be needed for the buffet.'

'It'll do you good to put your feet up for ten minutes,' Susan grinned, tripping behind her into the taverna with her fancy carrier-bag swinging from her arm. 'I just love those shoes, by the way. Thank you for sparing the time to come with me.'

Anna ordered two cups of coffee and a honey cake for Susan who sat munching it thoughtfully as she gazed out of the window at the passing crowd.

'I'm still worried about staying on,' she said, at last. 'I like the job and I suppose I would have difficulty finding another one quite so lucrative if I went back to England but it can't last much longer than a year. Once Martha is a little older and things are more settled she will be going off to boarding school, I expect, and that will mean good-bye to Susan Loftus! Andreas didn't make any promises when he hired me.'

Anna gazed at her across the table. 'Andreas?' she said. 'I thought it would have been Martha's mother who would have made that sort of decision.'

'He was on the spot at the time. Our Man in London, so to speak.' Susan drank the remainder of her coffee.

'Mrs Warrender wanted her daughter's minder to be English, you see, so Andreas advertised and—there I was! I think he preferred me to someone older as a companion for Martha. I don't know.' She gazed into her empty cup. 'One never does with Andreas,' she added after a moment's thought. 'He's the complete enigma, like the Sphinx, thinking deeply behind that noble brow of his without even flickering an eyelid and giving nothing away. But you must recognise that even better than I do,' she suggested with an oblique glance in Anna's direction. 'You've known him for a long time.'

'A long time ago,' Anna said, gathering her parcels together. 'Andreas, the adolescent, and Andreas, the grown man, appear to be different.'

'Why don't you like him?' Susan demanded. 'Because I can see you don't.'

Anna flushed scarlet. 'It's not just a question of liking,' she answered. 'It—goes deeper than that, but I'd rather not talk about it, Susan, if you don't mind.'

'I think you must have been in love with him at one time,' Susan suggested outrageously. 'Is that why you treat him so coldly now? He didn't leave you in the lurch when he went off to conquer the world, did he?'

Anna got to her feet, moving to the counter to pay the bill. 'No, we weren't in love,' she said steadily enough. 'We were good friends once upon a time.'

'That's fatal!' Susan declared, her roguish eyes full of laughter. 'Seriously, though, I wonder if he'll marry Lara Warrender when the time comes. Lara may even be buying this villa in the mountains with that in mind.' She paused in the doorway, looking up and down the street. 'I want to buy a pair of decent sun-specs,' she announced. 'Where would you suggest? I want to make sure that I don't damage my eyes with anything cheap.'

Anna glanced pointedly at her wristwatch.

'If you want a good optician,' she said, 'I can take you round to Adolf Kanneti, but you may have to wait. He's a very busy man.'

'No problem!' Susan assured her. 'I have all morning till one o'clock.'

'I'll drive you to Nicolaides Street,' Anna offered, 'but I can't promise to wait.'

'Don't worry about me,' Susan said airily. 'I'll get the bus back, or a taxi. They seem to be all over the place.'

She chattered all the way back to the market where Anna had parked her car, although she did not mention Andreas again, probably thinking that she had already exhausted the subject as far as Anna was concerned. When they parted at the optician's she said breezily, 'Have fun! If you stumble upon anyone from the Crescent Beach I'll be back before one and I'm still all in one piece in spite of the heat!'

She vanished up the indoor stairs to the shop and Anna drove away wondering why the sunshine was suddenly less bright and the view across the bay clouded as if by rain.

When it was time to go to the Crescent Beach the following evening she found herself thinking of an excuse to stay away from the dinner-party which would include both Andreas and Lara Warrender, but she knew that it would only disappoint her mother if she refused to go.

'Mrs Warrender is such a beautiful person,' Dorothy remarked before they went up to dress, 'and she makes me feel relaxed. It would appear that Andreas owes a great deal to her influence and I'm sure he's grateful.'

Grateful and in love? Anna pressed her hands tightly against her sides as they went up in the lift. She could never have imagined Andreas in love like that—not for a reason, not out of gratitude at being helped up the ladder of success by a beautiful woman at least ten years his senior and the mother of a six-year-old child into the bargain, but these things happened, didn't they? The world, and love, and bitterness were all too complicated to understand.

'What will you wear?' Dorothy asked.

'I don't know.' Anna's voice was rough with suppressed emotion. 'Something blue, I suppose. I can't hope to compete with Mrs Warrender.'

As the lift stopped Dorothy said, 'You have youth on your side and I like you best in blue!'

They walked to the Crescent Beach along the road because it was already dark, arriving just before seven o'clock to be ushered into the vast hall by a doorman in an immaculate white uniform who seemed to be expecting them.

'Mrs Warrender is waiting in the lounge,' he informed them, but already Martha was half-way across the hall, greeting them with a vivid smile. 'I'm to stay up, just for this once!' she announced. 'How do you do?' she added politely if belatedly. 'There's a cabaret tonight and I can't wait to see it.'

Anna introduced her mother and they made their way across the polished floor to where Lara Warrender was waiting for them with Andreas by her side.

'Mama!' he said, taking Dorothy's hands in his. 'It's good to see you looking so well.' He kissed her on both cheeks. 'I was in Athens yesterday and I called in on John Malecos. He asked how you were and said to tell you he would come for that promised holiday one day.'

Dorothy blushed prettily. 'He is always promising but he never arrives!' she said. 'I suppose you found Athens much the same?'

'I hadn't much time to look around,' he told her, 'but the traffic seemed worse than ever. Everyone behind a steering-wheel in Athens seems hell-bent on suicide, to say nothing of the pedestrians!'

'I wouldn't like to live there,' Dorothy said as Lara greeted her. 'It's not at all like Cyprus.'

Andreas turned to Anna, at last. 'I wondered if you would come,' he said. 'I half expected you to find some excuse.'

'Why should I do that?' she asked defensively.

'Because you can't let the past go,' he said without

hesitation. 'You demand too much, Anna, and I'm not the sort of person who says "sorry" more than once.'

'I don't expect you to apologise to me,' she said under her breath, 'and I'm not here to argue. I suppose you were in Athens on business,' she added, turning their conversation to a less controversial subject. 'Was it very warm?'

'Very!' He turned as Susan made a tardy appearance from one of the lifts. 'I hear you had a shopping spree on your hands yesterday. Susan was most grateful, I understand. She feels she took up too much of your precious time.'

'I had it to spare.' Anna felt relieved as Susan joined them. 'It was a pleasant change from shopping for vegetables.'

'I got my specs,' Susan announced, shaking hands. 'You were quite right about Adolf. I've never met such an understanding man!'

'Susan is always meeting unusual people,' Lara said a trifle drily, 'but thank you for taking care of her, Anna. She really can be an innocent abroad on occasion.' She turned to Andreas. 'I think you could order our drinks now,' she suggested. 'I told Dino we would be in by seven.'

She was completely relaxed, the perfect hostess in the ideal setting, dressed wisely in a pale grey dinner gown which would not eclipse any of her guests, her single jewel the magnificent diamond she wore on the third finger of her left hand over her platinum wedding ring.

The décor of the Crescent Beach seemed to reflect her own good taste, with its arched ceilings and fine woodwork and the wide, deep sofas placed at intervals on the highly polished marble floor. Long windows overlooked the dark mystery of the lantern-lit terraces and the gleam of water beyond them, and somewhere close at hand an orchestra played.

'Well,' Andreas asked at Anna's elbow, 'what do you think of it?'

She looked up at him, disconcerted for a moment by his directness. 'The hotel? What do you expect me to say? It's wonderful—everything a four-star hotel should be,' she answered truthfully.

'Lara does the décor,' he said. 'She has excellent taste. What will you have to drink?'

'Sherry, please.'

'It used to be orange-juice!'

'I'm grown up now!'

'So you are. I should have noticed.'

'Andreas,' she begged, 'do you think we could—forget our differences just for tonight? After all, we are Lara's guests.'

'As you say.' He turned away with a brief smile to order their drinks. 'It will be a pleasant change. Lara has asked Nikos Masistas to join us, by the way,' he added. 'That should please you. They met on the tennis courts.'

Nikos joined them almost immediately, bowing over Lara's hand.

'A nice surprise!' he said, kissing Dorothy on both cheeks. 'Mrs Warrender plays tennis as she does everything else—magnificently!'

It was too extravagant, Anna thought, but Lara smiled at him. 'Flattery will get you nowhere,' she said. 'And why the formality? My name is Lara—to my friends. Thank you for all the help you've given me with the villa, Nikos,' she added more seriously. 'It is very kind of you.'

'Don't even think about it,' he said. 'I heard it was coming on to the market so I thought I would mention it when you told me what you wanted. I can make arrangements for you to inspect it whenever you like,' he offered.

Lara glanced at Andreas who had given his order to the bar attendant. 'Could we go quite soon?' she asked. 'Tomorrow, perhaps?'

'Tomorrow will be fine.' Andreas sat down beside her. 'I'll hire a car and we can take Martha and Susan with us. You'd like that, infant, wouldn't you?' he asked the adoring child who now sat on the arm of his chair smiling down at him.

Martha said, 'Oh, yes, please!' and Susan also smiled.

They were all so relaxed, Anna thought, sipping her drink as Nikos sat down beside her, just like one big, happy family now that they were to go off for a day into the mountains with nobody left behind.

'You didn't expect the pleasure of my company,' Nikos said, bending close, 'but I couldn't resist Lara's invitation when I knew you were going to be here. What made you change your mind about neglecting your duties at the villa for one whole evening, I wonder?'

'A desire to see what a four-star hotel was really like. How it functioned,' Anna laughed. 'It's—overwhelming!'

'You've never been here before?'

'Never.'

'Andreas is on to a good thing, I guess, getting a seat on the Board, but I suppose that was Lara's influence. She's very good to him, I hear.'

'He'll work quite hard in return,' Anna said, not wanting to discuss the relationship. 'You know the hotel quite well, of course.'

'It's practically my second home,' he agreed. 'I could have a flat, like Andreas, when I haven't work to do on the estate. When are you coming to see us, by the way?'

'When the summer rush is over,' Anna said. 'Your mother will understand.'

The head waiter came to stand beside Lara's chair. 'We are ready for you now, Madam, whenever it is convenient to you,' he said.

'We are so early because of Martha,' Lara explained. 'You understand?'

'Perfectly, Madam.'

Following Lara, they moved towards the restaurant resplendent in its décor of old rose and gold with little silk shades on the candles at the tables and pink linen tablecloths to match the rose-coloured carpet which covered the floor. The orchestra had started to play, but so far the small square of parquet in the centre of the room which served as a dance floor was unoccupied. Nobody wanted to dance this early in the evening and most of the tables were empty.

Lara indicated their seats and they sat down to study the extensive menu. Sitting between Andreas and Nikos, Anna was fascinated by the variety presented to them, making a mental calculation of the trouble and dedication it had taken in the kitchens. For there would be more than one kitchen, she supposed, with everything to hand to make the work easy.

'What are you thinking about?' Nikos asked.

'I was thinking how easy it would be to accept all this—everything going like clockwork because so many people are doing just one thing.'

'Don't you believe it!' Andreas said, listening on her other side. 'It was chaos this morning simply because someone had burnt a pan, and half-an-hour ago the second chef took umbrage over a sauce which was not exactly to his liking. It isn't all beer and skittles, by any means, simply because you have earned an extra star or two. Prestige can be an ugly word at times when the pressure is on.'

'But you love that sort of thing,' Anna pointed out. 'Otherwise, you wouldn't be doing it.'

He looked across the table at Lara. 'That's true,' he agreed. 'I've been trained in management and it suits me very well, but without Lara we wouldn't have all this perfection.'

The atmosphere was just right, and as the meal progressed a warmth of friendliness appeared to wrap them round. To her utter delight, Nikos asked Martha to dance after the main course had been served and they had ordered their sweet.

'She adores Nikos,' Lara smiled. 'He has been so kind to her, making her feel like an adult and helping her with her tennis. I think the coach overwhelms her a little and

Nikos treats it just as a game.'

'She could learn a lot from Nikos,' Andreas said. 'Anna, will you dance with me?' he asked, standing beside her chair.

'Of course, she will!' Lara assured him. 'She must know you do it rather well.'

Anna didn't know. All those years ago Andreas hadn't danced at all because he had never been keen to learn, preferring the outdoor life of the mountains where he could fish and shoot with her father's friends, but now everything about him seemed to be different. He held out his hand to her and she felt her fingers imprisoned in a commanding grip as he led her on to the dance floor.

'Does this surprise you so much?' he asked, putting his arm about her. 'It was also part of my training.'

'You are so utterly changed, I never thought of us dancing together,' she answered lamely.

'We've grown up, Anna.' His face was so very near her own, his arm tightening about her as they circled the floor. 'We are two entirely different people now and we can't pretend about it.'

'I never thought you would change,' she said uncertainly. 'I thought—it would always be the same, but I see now that would be impossible. You chose a different sort of life and we have been left behind.'

'Would you have come with me if I had asked you at the time?' he demanded. 'All those years ago would you have taken a chance and married me? All right, that wasn't a fair question,' he added quickly when she didn't answer him immediately. 'I should never have asked it because you have let me see the error of my ways in no uncertain manner and we can't put back the clock. I did what I did because I quarrelled with your father six years ago, but you are not willing to forgive, like your mother.'

She moistened her suddenly dry lips. 'No,' she said. 'It's something I just can't understand—a sort of betrayal. At one time we were all very close.'

'We could be that way again if you would only look at

things in their true perspective. I am here to stay, Anna, living on the same island, in the hotel next door, and it seems a pity that we can't live peaceably and without recrimination. I'll be managing the Crescent for Lara and you two could so easily be friends. She's a wonderful person, believe me, and already your mother has taken her to her heart. What is it with you that you can't accept us?'

She felt herself stiffen in his arms, her breath held as the dance came to an end. 'I have no place in your life,' she said. 'It could never be the same as it was before you went away.'

Nikos and his partner came across the floor to join them. 'Time for the cabaret,' Nikos said. 'Who is it tonight?'

'The Parlou Brothers. They do the circuit of six hotels,' Andreas explained. 'Their act is very good and Lara has engaged them for the rest of the season. We vary it with two dance groups and a ventriloquist for the children.'

The floor show was deft and accomplished. The two brothers danced into the middle of the parquet square in their tight-fitting black trousers and immaculate silk shirts to the quick tempo of the guitars and drums, circling and weaving their way across the highly polished wood with hardly a moment to draw breath between one dance and the next, and then, with the lights dimmed to enhance the tension, one of them put an upturned glass on the other's head. Anna had seen it done many times, but one glance at Martha convinced her that enchantment had been let loose for the little girl who often felt alone. She stood gazing, wide-eyed, as glass after glass was filled with the red wine of the island and built up, one on the other, into an unbelievable column fifteen glasses high while the dancing never stopped. Brother followed brother between the tables until, to her shy delight, she was invited to place the final glass in position.

'I'd let it fall!' she cried. 'I couldn't do it. I'd spoil everything!'

'Of course, you could do it!' Andreas encouraged her. 'Here we go! I'll help you.'

He lifted her into his arms and the delighted child placed the necessary card on top of the highest glass, her small, flushed face bright and anxious as she drew her hand away.

'I've done it!' she breathed. 'I've done it, Andreas!'

A small lighted candle was placed on Martha's card and the brothers took their bow.

'And now, to bed,' Lara said, kissing her daughter on the cheek as she finished the ice-cream which had almost melted in its silver dish as she had watched the cabaret. 'You've had your treat, so fall asleep at once and don't keep Susan upstairs too long. She likes to dance, too, you know.'

Obediently Martha wished them all good night, and when she came to Anna she whispered shyly, 'Can I come to your hotel tomorrow to see the little lighthouse?'

'You can come at any time,' Anna agreed willingly. 'It isn't far to walk along the beach.'

Martha was still clinging to Andreas' hand, unwilling to let it go.

'Come on, Marty,' he said. 'Don't keep Susan waiting.'

Their coffee was served as the orchestra began to play again. Nikos danced with Anna while Andreas lead Lara on to the floor and Dorothy sat alone at the table enjoying her role of spectator as the head waiter poured fresh coffee for her and brought liqueurs. Her mother was enjoying herself, Anna thought, as much as anyone.

It was after ten o'clock before they rose to go.

'It's been a wonderful evening,' Dorothy said. 'Perhaps you will come to the villa again before you leave for the mountains. We can't promise you dancing or a cabaret, but we have a folk singer who is really very good.'

'Which way are you going home?' Andreas asked. 'It's quicker by the shore and there's a full moon. I'll take you along the beach.'

Dorothy hesitated. 'Why not?' she said. 'It will be like old times walking across the sand.' They went arm-in-arm, Anna between Nikos and her mother; with Andreas on the outside.

'What was that song we used to sing?' Andreas asked. 'Something about getting home before the dawn.'

'You ought to remember it,' Dorothy laughed 'I can still hear you singing it at the top of your voice even over the sound of the sea.'

Anna knew what it was, but she could not bring herself to sing it, not there on the quiet beach with the moonlight silvering the waves and Andreas' little lighthouse winking steadily ahead of them, pointing the way home.

When they reached the terrace he turned to go back with Nikos and Susan, and for a moment Anna saw his face in full moonlight. It was the face she had known all these years ago, but suddenly the eyes were hard.

'Will you come in for a nightcap?' her mother asked.

He shook his head. 'You know what hotels are like,' he said. 'I must get back.' He bent to kiss her on both cheeks. 'Sleep well, Mama,' he said. 'I think you have enjoyed yourself.'

He did not look at Anna, and when she turned towards the villa there was no more bitterness in her heart.

CHAPTER FOUR

THE busiest day of the week for the Villa Severus was Wednesday. Most of their guests were elderly and preferred to travel then to avoid the turmoil of Saturday and Sunday when other holidaymakers flew in to Larnaca from Britain and Europe. The Americans arrived at any time because they were generally on a tour of the Middle East, and the Greeks hardly came at all.

Added to all this was the fact that the excavations for

the new swimming-pool had begun in earnest, with a mechanical digger chugging away industriously out of sight behind a canvas screen. There was a confusion of noise which most of the guests seemed to accept philosophically with the exception of the elderly Mrs Pope who was heard to remark that they 'might as well be in Piccadilly Circus'. This caused a smile but little comment from the other guests who considered the pool an amenity they could very well enjoy on their next visit to the Severus.

Anna worried about the upheaval but felt that it was something they could not avoid if the pool was to be in operation by June, and certainly the contractors were doing their best to cause as little inconvenience as possible. The digger, they assured her, would be gone within two days.

Her mother took a great deal of interest in the work going on, reporting to her in the office before each meal. She also mentioned that Martha had been an interested onlooker as the digger scooped out the rich brown earth on the far side of the screen.

'She is a very intelligent child,' Dorothy remarked, 'but lonely. I fear that Susan is rather neglectful.'

'Doesn't Susan come over here with her?' Anna asked, surprised.

'Not always. But then I expect Martha often wanders off on her own. There can't be much amusement for a small girl who is naturally inquisitive in a large four-star hotel like the Crescent Beach where everyone lies around on the beach most of the day covered in sun-tan oil and dances far into the night. She enjoys the cabarets, though, when she is allowed to stay up to see them.'

'Her mother is here on business,' Anna pointed out 'That's why Susan is here.'

'If you ask me,' Dorothy returned drily, 'that young woman is here specifically for her own amusement. I see her walking along the beach with a different man in tow most days, obviously forgetting all about the child.'

Anna signed a final letter.

'Mama!' You're fast becoming the village gossip,' she laughed 'It isn't your style.'

'I don't like to see children neglected,' Dorothy said, 'and it annoys me to see people exploited. Mrs Warrender is paying that young woman to look after her daughter—quite handsomely, I suspect—and she isn't doing her job.'

'Did Martha come over this morning?' Anna asked 'I thought I heard her voice.'

Dorothy nodded. 'We had our usual little walk along the mole,' she smiled. 'It always makes me think of you and Andreas toddling out there before Andreas was big enough to help your father build the little lighthouse. It seems to fascinate Martha when she sees it winking in the dark, and no doubt Andreas has told her all about finding the suitable stones to match it with the wall. She wondered if they would dig up more stones at the swimming-pool. They are going rather deep.'

'I suppose they have to make the proper foundations,' Anna said, thinking more about those long-ago walks along the tiny harbour wall than the pool they needed so much. 'There must be six feet, at least, at the deep end where we will have the diving-board, so the digger will have to go much deeper than that.'

'It's quite fascinating,' Dorothy admitted, 'although I'll miss my trees.'

'We can plant some more—between the pool and Candy's Place,' Anna pointed out, 'just in case Andreas changes his mind.'

'About Candy's Place?' Dorothy looked at her in surprise. 'I thought he meant to keep it just as it is for a bit of atmosphere.'

'That's what he says at the moment, but if it comes to making a great deal of money he might think differently,' Anna said. 'Candy's Place is one of the prime sites along the bay now that the big appartment blocks are closing in on us from the Limassol end.'

'If he has made a promise he will keep it,' Dorothy declared. 'He has changed now—changed completely.'

'I want to agree with you,' Anna said. 'I want to agree with you so much and I know that he has changed, but I think he has become hard and determined now, not looking back at the past with any sort of kindness. Only looking to the future and the full life he will lead.'

'Has he spoken about the future to you?' Dorothy's eyes were anxious.

'Why should he? Mama, he has come back after six years an utterly different person,' Anna said 'and I am no longer his confidante.'

'As you used to be,' Dorothy sighed.

'We were children.' Anna's heart was suddenly heavy in her breast. 'Everything changes.'

'I think things could be the same again if we tried a little harder.'

'Oh, Mama, you were always an optimist, and always forgiving!'

They ate their lunch in a preoccupied silence, although Anna knew that her mother's thoughts were still in the past and on the conversation they had just had. Dorothy wanted to forget the years between when she had suffered so much disappointment and sorrow. She wanted to wipe the slate clean and start again, but could that ever happen? The years had changed them all, and Andreas more than anyone.

'I'll have my little rest,' Dorothy said as they walked from the buffet bar adjoining the terrace. 'Do you have to work this afternoon?'

'Only for an hour till I finish the letters.' Anna halted at the office door. 'Would you like a run into Limassol when the shops open again at three o'clock?'

'That would be nice,' Dorothy agreed. 'I'll take a little stroll first and perhaps Martha will come over to have another look at the digger. It seems to keep her enthralled.'

'Don't stand about too long in the heat,' Anna warned,

'and take a hat with you. I'll come for you at half-past three.'

An hour and several interruptions later, she sat back from her typewriter surveying what was left of the pile of correspondence on her desk, deciding that it could wait because it was almost too hot to work, even in the office.

Crossing to the open window she became aware of an unaccustomed silence, the sound of the busy digger no more than an echo beyond the garden trees. No doubt the excavation was finished, as the contractor had promised, in record time, but the silence seemed intense, blotting out everything. She walked to the door, coming into the brilliant sunshine which dazzled the beach and the blue-green water beyond until the sound of men's voices came rushing towards her, urgent, harsh, demanding. Paris came running from behind the canvas screen, white-faced and dishevelled, his clothes covered in grey dust, his eyes widely alarmed. She ran then, meeting him half-way, clutching at his shoulder in an effort to calm him.

'Paris, what is it? What has gone wrong?'

He stared at her for a split second without answering, shock taking away his immediate power of speech.

'Paris!' She looked beyond him to the screen where other men were appearing. 'What has happened?'

'Your mother,' he said, clutching at his throat as if to tear the words out. 'She has fallen. There has been an accident and all the ground caved in.'

Anna did not wait for details, running as fast as her trembling limbs would carry her towards the canvas screen.

'The little girl,' Paris said, running beside her. 'She will be all right.'

But not my mother! Not Mama, who is so frail from all those years of sickness and defeat. What could have happened? What could possibly have gone wrong?

Before she could reach the screen the contractor came swiftly towards her.

'Could you phone for a doctor?' he asked urgently.

'And perhaps an ambulance.'

Anna attempted to pass him.

'I must go to my mother! She will need me and I have to be there with her—to see her.'

'There's nothing to see,' he told her gently. 'The ground just gave way as we had finished digging and she was standing there with the little girl. Nobody could have done a thing, Miss Rossides—it just happened. One minute we had stopped work and the next there was a great, gaping hole beneath the foundations. Please try to get a doctor,' he urged. 'We are doing all we can back there, I assure you, and we'll get her out, but a doctor could be essential in the circumstances. It will be easy enough to phone from the villa.'

Easy? Yes, it would be easy to phone. She ran back along the terrace with Paris panting at her heels.

'Get blankets, Paris, and some brandy,' she commanded. 'Ask in the bar . . .' She reached the office, dialling the well-known number automatically, her fingers trembling with urgency while the fatal words rushed round in her head. 'She has fallen. Your mother has fallen . . . There has been an accident. All the ground just fell away . . .'

There had been no sound, the rumbling of an earth tremor which was often felt on that erratic coastline or an eruption from some other cause—nothing!

And no sound, either, from the instrument she held in her hand. The line was dead, cut off somewhere by fallen rubble or cascading earth.

She was half-way to the Crescent Beach before she realised that her high-heeled shoes were sinking into the sand, impeding her progress in her frantic attempt at rescue. Kicking them off, she left them on the beach, running freely now but still half blinded by the tears she could not shed. People were sitting on the rocks when she came to the wall, people in bright costumes under the blue and white umbrellas, people laughing, people enjoying themselves in the bright sunshine and nobody aware of what had happened on the other side of that dividing wall.

Climbing it without difficulty, she threw herself on to the sand on the far side, running blindly up the beach where someone rose languidly from a chair.

'Do you need nelp?'

She did not hear the question, running on until another man caught her in his arms.

'Anna, where are you going?' Andreas demanded. 'What has happened?'

'It's Mama!' She used the old, well-beloved name automatically, the name they had both used as children all these years ago. 'We have to have a doctor. I tried to telephone from the villa but the line was dead—cut off when the earth fell in——'

He took her completely into his arms, holding her for a moment with a tenderness which soothed the wild tumult in her heart before he led her quickly towards the hotel.

'Try to tell me what happened,' he commanded as they mounted the terrace steps. 'As much as you can without the details.'

'It was at the swimming-pool. The digger had been working all day and there was a lot of noise, but they hoped to finish before six. Mama must have gone to see how it looked——' She turned to face him, her eyes wide in her pale, anguished face. 'Andreas, they were both there—Mama and Martha.'

'Martha? What happened to her?'

'She's safe, I think. Paris said she would be all right.'

His jaw tightened. 'She said she was going to visit your mother. I told her not to be long.' They had reached the vast entrance hall which was mercifully empty at that time of day. 'We'll get them out, Anna—don't worry,' he said. 'If you want to go back to the villa I'll follow you after I've phoned.'

She turned blindly back across the crowded terraces where people were drinking tea and iced orange-juice, back to the wall and along the beach on the other side where her shoes were still lying on the sand, but she did not seem to see them, two scraps of pink canvas lying there beside the water with the wind blowing over them.

By the time she reached the excavations a small crowd had gathered, but Paris was keeping the too-inquisitive back, allowing only the workmen to enter with the spades they had abandoned when the mechanical digger went to work.

'Paris——?'

He shook his head.

'Not yet, but we will find your mother. The little girl has been taken to the house,' he added. 'She is not hurt.'

'I'll go to her soon.'

Her mother was uppermost in her thoughts as she pushed her way through the crowd, seeing that the contractor was there, standing on the edge of what seemed to be a great chasm and looking down in perplexity at what he saw. Anna ran to his side...

'Mr. Zacharakis——?'

He turned towards her, outlined against the gaping hole where his digger had sank.

'It is terrible,' he said. 'Incomprehensible! It all just caved in while we were standing there, looking on. We've done all we can, but it looks as if there were other, earlier excavations, like those farther along the coast, and the ground just gave way.'

'My mother——?'

'She's down there.' He looked stricken. 'Poor lady! She did her best to shield the child, but a beam fell across her—the lintel of a door, perhaps, although we can't be sure till we've cleared away the rubble.'

'Mr. Zacharakis—do you think she is still alive?' Anna whispered.

'Most certainly, she is,' he said, patting her arm, 'but we must not move her until we make sure that nothing else will fall, you understand?'

Andreas pushed his way through the bewildered crowd.

'Martha is at the villa. She's all right,' Anna assured him.

'And Mama?'

'She's—down there.' Anna was still gazing into the cavity. 'Oh, Andreas. she could be hurt—seriously hurt. Why had this to happen to her, of all people?'

Without answering, he moved to the edge of the crater, followed by the contractor and two workmen carrying spades. Dazed, she watched as they eased themselves over the edge, inch by careful inch, while far beneath them, deep beyond the excavated swimming-pool, a silence reigned which seemed to engulf the whole world.

How long she waited there while the men worked she did not know, but presently she heard the banshee wail of an ambulance siren and the doctor Andreas had summoned was by her side. She knew him well; he had brought her into the world over twenty years ago, helping her mother through a difficult birth.

'Doctor Ioannu——'

He kissed her cheek

'Go back to the villa,' he said.

'They are both down there, my mother and Andreas.'

'I know. I will see that they come to no harm.'

'They could both be dead. He took a risk—'

'I do not think they are dead. Andreas is a strong man and your mother has a will to live. I know that from experience, but you must help me. The ambulance is here but we may have to take them both to the villa first. Get blankets, and hot soup for the others, and you must look after the little girl till her mother arrives.'

'I'll—do what I can.' Reluctantly she turned away. 'Will you send for me if—if anything happens?'

'I will send for you,' he promised kindly. 'It may be a long job, Anna, or we could get them both out without difficulty. I have much experience of such accidents. Trust me.'

Of course, she trusted him! What else could she do when the pain in her heart was so intense, tearing her apart? The two people she loved most in all the world were down there at the mercy of the past where a stone pillar from a bygone age might fall across them, killing them immediately. She had no doubt now that Hugh Zacharakis had stumbled upon an ancient settlement close to the shore or an isolated homestead disturbed by the excavations he had made for her ambitious swimming-pool.

The two people she loved most in all the world! The poignant words haunted her as she ran back along the terrace and on to the arched loggia where guests and staff had gathered since the arrival of the ambulance at the main door. How long had it taken her to realise that she was in love with Andreas—that she had always been in love with him?

While he, in his turn, was in love with Lara!

She took Lara's daughter in her arms as the little girl ran towards her, kissing her cheek.

'Everything will be all right, Martha,' she soothed her. 'Your mother will soon be here.'

There was a confusion of questions as the guests gathered round, offers of help and advice which she didn't really hear.

'Don't go down there,' she pleaded. 'You could risk your life.'

That's what Andreas was doing—Andreas and Hugh Zacharakis and the doctor. They were putting themselves in danger to bring her mother out alive. Her heart turned over at the thought.

'What can we do here?' someone asked.

Instantly she was calm, issuing directions, finding a spare room in case anyone else should be hurt in the rescue attempt, sending Paris to the Crescent Beach to try to locate Martha's mother or even Susan, who must be somewhere around.

Susan came running across the sand, excusing herself

as usual. 'I thought, when she was visiting your mother, I could just read for a while,' she said, 'and I had some washing to do.'

Or someone to meet, Anna thought, but without bitterness.

'Where is Mrs Warrender?' she demanded. 'Is she in the hotel?'

'She's at a meeting.' Susan paused on the loggia, breathless. 'It was something quite important and she wasn't to be disturbed—something to do with the hotel.'

'Go back and find her,' Anna said, 'Tell her Martha is safe but I'm keeping her over here till Doctor Ioannu can see her.'

'And—your mother?'

'We don't know.' Anna looked towards the canvas screen the contractor had erected to keep the dust from drifting across the loggia. 'Andreas is down there, helping to get her out.'

'Andreas?' Susan murmured. 'Oh, my God! Are they in danger? Mrs Warrender will never forgive me. It isn't only Martha now.'

'You tell her,' Anna said firmly.

Lara would come, standing where she had stood a moment ago looking down into the dark crater where her love might have ended, Lara whose eyes were already saddened by memories of the past.

When Susan had gone she went to comfort Martha, but the child was already asleep, wrapped in blankets on one of the settees in the private sitting-room with a hint of a smile on her lips like the sleeping Eros of Paphos, her short golden curls tossed on the pillow Elli had placed beneath her head.

No need to wait beside her, Anna thought. Martha was safe until Lara came to claim her daughter.

Running, she made her way back to the scene of the excavations where the ambulance men were waiting with stretchers and first-aid. Two stretchers, she noticed, shivering.

'They're getting them out,' Paris said. 'We thought Andreas might be trapped when some more stone fell, but it is not so. He is able to speak to the doctor.'

Anna pressed forward without answering him.

'You mustn't go too near,' Paris cautioned. 'The earth just seems to slip away.'

Slowly, almost effortlessly, it seemed, men were reaching down to receive a burden while one of the stretchers was passed along to them. She saw the doctor's head and shoulders apear above the cavity and then Andreas, covered in white dust, as if in a shroud.

She could not go to him; she could not help in any way because of the danger of falling rubble, but he looked directly at her as he was helped out, willing her the courage she could not find for herself. When he reached her she was trembling.

'It's all right, we've got her out,' he said quietly. 'She's unconscious but she's alive.'

Anna clung to him, unable to voice her relief and the tremendous debt she owed him while he held her for a moment with the same tenderness hc had shown once before, which was surely compassion. He knew how she felt about her mother, and by the tightness of his jaw and the look in his eyes she knew that he felt the same. For a fleeting instant he was the old Andreas she had loved in the past and still loved.

The ambulance men were bringing her mother out, laying her carefully on the stretcher with a red blanket over her while the doctor took her pulse. Curiously enough, it was the vivid colour of the blanket which held Anna's attention—red, like blood.

Andreas' arm was still firmly about her shoulders.

'They will take her to the hospital,' he said. 'It is the best thing to do. She is still unconscious.'

'You saved her life.' She scarcely heard her own words of gratitude. 'We will always remember that.'

'Someone else would have done it if I hadn't,' he said. 'All we must think of now is Mama.'

Frail and heartrendingly pale in the bright sunlight, her mother was carried past her.

'I must go with her. Surely they will let me go in the ambulance?' she said, freeing herself at last.

'Doctor Ioannu will arrange everything,' he told her, 'and if it isn't possible, Anna, I will take you.'

She said, 'You must look after Martha till her mother gets here. She's asleep in the little sitting-room.'

'Which is the best thing that could have happened.' His mouth was suddenly grim. 'Thank you for taking care of her, Anna. She is very precious.'

They followed the stretcher round the gable end of the villa, through the rose garden Dorothy had tended lovingly for most of her married life, to the waiting ambulance at the front door. The doctor was already there.

'You can go with her.' He had answered her question before it was asked. 'She may regain consciousness on the way.'

As the stretcher was slid carefully inside, a woman in a pale dress ran through the entrance gates. It was Lara in search of her daughter. Andreas went immediately to her side and she flung both arms about his neck in heartfelt gratitude.

'Andreas, my dear, how will I ever repay you!' she cried. 'You have saved my child and you know how much she means to me.'

'Don't thank me,' he said. 'She was rescued before I got there—by the workmen—and she is now at the villa, safe and sound.'

Lara's eyes remained steady on his for a long, intimate moment while Anna stumbled into the ambulance to sit down on the seat beside the stretcher, her own eyes suddenly dimmed with tears.

There was a vagueness about the next two hours which made nothing of time. Once her mother was safely in the white hospital bed and had opened her eyes in full consciousness to smile at her the world seemed to revolve again, although time had no place in it.

'It was a silly thing to do,' Dorothy whispered. 'We were standing too near to the edge and when the little one slipped I had to get her.' She gazed anxiously round the white-walled room. 'Is she here?'

'She is fast asleep at the villa or—or with her mother and Andreas at the Crescent Beach.'

'Andreas got me out. I thought I heard him say that Martha wasn't hurt just before everything turned black for me.' Dorothy moved her head uncertainly, looking towards the door. 'Do you think he will come?'

'Of course he will,' Anna assured her, 'but now you must get some sleep. I'll stay with you.'

Dorothy smiled. 'You are all very good to me. Do you think I have broken something?' she added drowsily. 'My back feels very—fragile.'

It was an old family joke, uttered poignantly at this time of crisis. They had all felt 'fragile' in the past when they didn't want to do something in particular.

'You will soon be well,' was all Anna could say as she took the thin hand in hers and prepared to wait.

She sat in an ante-room just outside the ward door while two consultants conferred with Doctor Ioannu and presently the old family doctor came to reassure her. Her mother had escaped serious injury, although three of her ribs had been crushed by falling stone.

'We will keep her here for a couple of weeks,' he decided. 'She's very frail, Anna, and the rest will do her good. I have to be honest and say that I think the hotel is too much for her and she does not take kindly to the heat of summer down here on the coast. Ideally, she should be able to go into the mountains during the summer months, at least.'

It was something Anna had realised for a long time, something she would dearly have loved to do for the woman who had cared for her all her life, but circumstances had been against her. Now, when it was so important, she would have to think of some way to carry out Doctor Ioannu's advice.

It grew dark as she listened for the sound of a car bringing Andreas to her mother's bedside, although he had not made her such a promise. He had offered to take her to the hospital if she could not go in the ambulance, but that was all.

When he came she was ready to leave and her mother was asleep.

'Best to leave her,' she said. 'She needs sleep more than anything else. She had three crushed ribs, but the doctors have strapped her up and she is now comfortable. I think—if you wanted to look in at her—they would let you.'

He held out his hand. 'We'll go together,' he said.

Standing by her mother's bedside with Andreas it seemed as if the years had rolled away and they were boy and girl together again. Time, which had parted them, stood aside and there was only the joy of sharing in her heart. That it was too late now did not occur to her for a moment as he pressed her hand in sympathy.

'We must talk about this when we get back to the villa,' he said quietly. 'We have a decision to make.'

We? She would have bridled at the word twenty-four hours ago, but now it seemed only natural that Andreas should make decisions for them, at least where her mother was concerned. Tall and purposeful, he was taking the situation into his own hands because, for a moment, he had seen her weakness and recognised her need.

He drove her back to the villa where the contractor's men were still clearing up the debris at the swimming-pool, working under floodlights which they had erected at the terrace edge.

'You know that this will mean the end of your pool,' he said as they stood on the loggia to watch. 'The cave-in will have to be reported—Hugh Zacharakis will do that as the contractor—and the authorities will step in to see what further excavation reveals.'

'What do you think they will find?' she asked anxiously.

He shrugged. 'Some Roman remains, I expect. They were here for three hundred years, remember.'

Anna drew in a deep breath. 'It would be futile to argue,' she agreed in some dismay. 'What do the authorities do in a case like this?'

'They wouldn't pull down the villa, you can rest assured about that. Half the island is built on old foundations and we might only have found an ancient tomb, but they'll want to dig for artefacts to make quite sure. My guess is a villa of some sort when it is so close beside the sea.' He stood looking at her, his gaze thoughtful for a moment. 'It could make a difference, Anna, either way. If it is a large find it could attract tourists; if it is only a segregated tomb it would be walled round and preserved, with an access to the public and that would be all.'

'What are you hoping for?' she asked.

'A few bronze coins with an emperor's head on one side and a temple of Aphrodite on the reverse. It happens all the time,' he declared lightly.

'It could mean the end of the Villa Severus as we know it,' she pointed out.

'I don't think so.' He took her by the arm. 'And if it did it needn't be the end of the world as far as you are concerned.'

She felt a hard lump rising in her throat. 'It's been my home for as long as I can remember,' she reminded him. 'All I've ever dreamed about could have happened within these walls, but—but I don't suppose you can understand that.'

He gripped her by the shoulders, turning her to face the light. 'Sometimes we have to make adjustments,' he said briefly, 'and not always in the way we would like. I hope you can keep the villa, but you may have to give up the idea of expanding it as an hotel. It's in the lap of the gods, isn't it?' he added with a faint smile.

She thought about Lara and the child they both cherished. 'Lara will have taken Martha back to the Crescent Beach,' she said, 'and you must want to go. I won't keep you.'

He looked beyond her to the small group of holiday-makers gathering for drinks before dinner at the terrace bar.

'Things seem to be going smoothly enough,' he agreed. 'I'll see you in the morning in case you need my help. At least I could stand in for you while you visit the hospital.'

She held out her hand. 'How can I thank you, Andreas?' she asked. 'How can I ever repay you for all you have done?'

He smiled crookedly, raising her fingers to his lips in a gesture of mock gallantry. 'I did it for Mama,' he said. 'Not for you, Anna.'

He walked away along the loggia and down the terrace steps while she stood watching in the starlight, tall, loose-limbed and attractive, the only man she had ever truly loved. There was no resentment in her heart now, only a great emptiness when she thought of the way ahead, of all the days and all the years when she would remember him walking away like this, out of her life for ever, perhaps. It was hard to accept the inevitable, but she knew that he had changed.

Nikos came hot on the heels of Andreas' leaving. 'I heard about the accident in Limassol,' he said, kissing her on both cheeks 'What happened?'

'When they were excavating for the swimming-pool the ground gave way. My mother and Lara's daughter went down with the rubble but they are both safe, thanks to Andreas. I think my mother tried to shield Martha with her own body when a plinth or something fell on them,' Anna explained.

'It could be another of these damned temples,' Nikos guessed. 'They're all over the place. Does it mean that the pool will be a no-go area till they're sure?'

'I'm afraid so.' She walked with him towards the bar.

'There's a ruined wall and some steps so they're sure to explore further. Andreas believes it might be another villa—a Roman one—and that would mean terraces and gardens and perhaps a tomb.'

'All those years ago,' he mused. 'Makes you think, doesn't it? They were just like us—building their walls and working hard and having children and a home life with a temple or two in their gardens and, perhaps, a tomb. If it wasn't a settlement that may be all they'll find—an ancient villa by the sea with a few bits of pottery scattered about and a coin or two thrown in for good measure.'

'That may be all,' she agreed. 'We'll just have to wait and see.'

'It's been a disappointment to you,' he guessed, 'but don't worry about it, Anna. Everything will work out for the best. How long do you think your mother will be in hospital?'

'At least two weeks.' Her smile faded. 'If only this hadn't happened to her, Nikos! She has suffered shock and she is so frail. Doctor Ioannu thinks she shouldn't be here during the summer months because of the heat.'

'In that case, you must bring her to the mountains,' he suggested, summoning Paris to order drinks. 'What will you have, Anna? You look so pale it will have to be something strong.'

She shook her head. 'I'd rather go straight in for a meal,' she decided. 'Can I persuade you to join me?'

'No persuasion needed!' he declared. 'But we will drink champagne. You are in need of it.'

They found an empty table overlooking the bay and suddenly it all seemed very unreal to Anna to be sitting there with Nikos eating the meal she had helped to prepare that morning when there was hardly a cloud on her horizon and the future had been full of hope.

'Anna,' he said when their coffee had been served, 'I meant what I said. When she is well enough you must bring your mother to the mountains. We can easily arrange that,' he added. 'Take her to Stroumbi. My mother will be only too pleased to have her.'

She turned towards him, unable to accept his offer although her heart was full of gratitude. 'I couldn't make a convenience of your family, Nikos,' she protested.

'Why not?' He covered her fingers with a warm, brown hand, leaning towards her. 'I want you to belong to it, I want you to be one of my family, Anna, more than anything else, and your mother would be safe with us.'

'I know.' She gazed down at the pink tablecloth. 'I know you would be kind to her, but I can't make that sort of decision. Not yet.'

'You will have to think of it before very long,' he pointed out. 'You will also have to think about the future of the villa. It's too much for you on your own.'

'I can manage,' she said. 'And, after all, it is our home.'

When they took a second cup of coffee out to the lounge Lara was coming across the hall from the front door.

'I had to come over to thank you,' she declared. 'You have been so kind to Martha and we owe so much to your mother. She saved my child.'

'Andreas had a hand in it, too,' Anna reminded her. 'If he hadn't come on the scene so quickly things could have been so different. As it is——'

'As it is your mother is in hospital and I feel very guilty.' Lara's large, expressive eyes were true mirrors of her genuine concern. 'I wonder if we can do anything for her—bring her to the Crescent Beach or something like that. We have several private suites.'

'That wouldn't do,' Anna said quickly. 'She has all the comfort necessary at the hospital and excellent medical care. Thank you for suggesting it, though. She will appreciate your offer.'

'I must go and visit her,' Lara decided. 'Do you think tomorrow, if she is well enough? Andreas would take me. I'm sure he will also want to go.'

'Yes.' Anna looked down at her empty cup. 'Will you

take some coffee with us, Lara?' she asked. 'I know you dine early.'

'We dine whenever we have time!' Lara laughed. 'We're not at the Crescent Beach on holiday, Andreas and I, and you know how busy you can be trying to work out all the problems of a busy hotel at one time. Without Andreas I could do very little at present. He has been— what is it you say?—a tower of strength to me these past two years.'

'Have you found your villa in the mountains yet?' Nikos asked signalling to Paris for more coffee. 'We are curious to know where you will settle.'

Lara shook her head. 'We have looked at one or two but have not yet decided,' she said. 'Andreas thinks that Pedhoulas or Prodhromos would be best for us because they are both very high and very beautiful. I could look all day at that wonderful view over the mountains to the Cedar Valley, and while we were there the cherry trees were still in bloom. They were like a white sea, stretching for miles.'

'You would not be far from us in the Marathasa Valley,' Nikos told her, 'although the roads through the mountains are not very good. If you decide to come farther west I'm sure we could help.'

There was the slightest pause before Lara answered. 'You are very kind offering your help, Nikos, but— perhaps we won't be visiting very much.' The latent sadness in her eyes deepened as she looked out through the long windows to the night sky beyond. 'We will be going there for a rest and the wonderful mountain air.'

'If you change your mind,' Nikos said, not knowing whether to feel snubbed or not, 'you can always call on us. As a matter of fact,' he added confidentially, 'I have just been trying to persuade Anna to bring her mother to Stroumbi to recuperate. We live outside the town and it is very beautiful there.'

Lara looked surprised. 'And will you go?' she asked Anna. 'Andreas is always saying how much you value your home.'

'I couldn't leave here for any length of time,' Anna said. 'Even though the swimming-pool may not be possible now I mean to keep the hotel going.'

'Of course!' Lara gazed at her inquisitively. 'Is it really what you want to do?'

'It's what I have to do.' Anna was remembering that first tentative take-over bid Andreas had made. 'It will never be a great money-spinner but it is what we wanted to achieve—an hotel which is more like a home.'

Lara's eyes sharpened. 'It has much potential, as you surely must know.' The shrewd businesswoman had taken over completely. 'This site is just right for expansion and perhaps you should think about it.'

'No,' Anna assured her, 'it wouldn't make any difference. I have no desire to expand—or to sell,' she added firmly.

Lara shrugged, smiling once more. 'It is your own decision, my dear, but if you should change your mind in the near future . . .'

'I'm sure I won't,' Anna assured her. 'When my mother is fit again we will carry on as we always have done, although I will try to send her to the mountains during the summer months.'

'You will need help during that time,' Lara pointed out, 'and Andreas will be at the Crescent Beach for the greater part of the summer. I'm sure he would be glad to help you.'

Anna got quickly to her feet. 'I couldn't possibly ask him,' she said.

'Why not?' Lara rose to go. 'He knows everything there is to know about the trade, and he has served a good apprenticeship.'

'Anna will be all right on her own,' Nikos said quickly. 'She has many friends to fall back on here on the island.'

'I'm sure she has,' Lara acknowledged, 'and Andreas is also one of them, is he not? He will be most willing to do what he can.'

Anna walked with them across the hall. 'Thank you for coming,' she said to Lara. 'Give my love to Martha and I hope she will soon get over her shock.'

'She'll be all right in the morning,' Lara said. 'You know what children are like, but I must really insist that Susan doesn't neglect her duties in future. She is here to look after Martha and also to teach her the rudiments of English and arithmatic before she goes off to school in Switzerland some time next year. That is another reason for the villa in the mountains,' she added. 'There are too many distractions for them in a large hotel.'

'Will you settle permanently in Cyprus?' They had reached the main door and Nikos held it open. 'Do you mean to make the new villa your home?'

Lara's eyes took on an added brightness. 'It's my fondest wish,' she admitted. 'It is many years since I had an established home of my own.'

'Always the businesswoman!' Nikos remarked as she disappeared into the night. 'Perhaps I should have escorted her back along the road, but I wanted to speak to you, Anna. I've phoned my parents about your mother's accident and they will be visiting her at the hospital. Try to convince her to come to Stroumbi and we will look after her for you.'

She paused at the office door, the tears so near her eyes that she could not look at him.

'You are all so kind,' she said. 'I'm sure she will want to come to you for a little while.'

'For as long as she needs to,' Nikos said firmly. 'We are very old friends.'

When she was finally in her own room with the door closed between her and the outside world, she crossed to her window, stepping out on to the narrow balcony which overlooked the sea. Couples in their summer clothes were strolling along the terrace, hand in hand, and farther along the sandy beach other couples, arms entwined, were walking by the water's edge blissfully happy in each other's company as they gazed at the stars and thought about a happy future. She had never felt so much alone in all her life, yet she had made decisions in the past when everything seemed to be going wrong, making them for her mother as well as herself, but now it seemed that Dorothy's decision whether to return home or retreat to the mountains would affect her future, too. Nikos wants her to go so much, she thought, and really it would be the best thing to do.

She would not think of Andreas nor of Lara, who was most surely his latest love. Lara had done so much for him so how could he not love her? She was beautiful, talented and kind, with so much to offer him, and now she was buying a villa in the mountains to be near him until they could eventually marry.

Was there a barrier, she wondered, something that might keep them apart for a little while—like a divorce, perhaps?

She thrust the suggestion aside, not wanting to think of it.

CHAPTER FIVE

THERE was much coming and going around the swimming-pool excavation next morning. Officials from Limassol and Nicosia had been alerted and the site was to be further explored, but it did not seem that much of importance had been found.

Andreas had come across from the Crescent Beach to go round with them.

'How long will they be, do you think?' Anna asked when they had not left by twelve o'clock. 'I've phoned the hospital and promised to go in.'

'I phoned earlier,' he said, glancing at his watch. 'I said we would be in this afternoon. They want her to rest.'

She hesitated. 'Andreas, you needn't worry about me

getting in to Limassol if you have something else to do,'
she said. 'I can take the pick-up and be back in time for
the dinner scramble.'

'That won't be necessary,' he said in the arbitrary tone
he sometimes adopted when she was being obstructive.
'I'll be going, anyway. Can you be ready by three
o'clock?'

She nodded. 'I'll take her some fruit. Oh, dear!' she
added in a careful undertone as Mrs Pope swooped on
them from across the hall. 'Good morning, Mrs Pope,'
she offered politely. 'Where are you bound for today?'

'I was bound for your office,' the good lady informed
her vehemently, 'but since you are here I'll make my
complaint right away.' She glanced in Andreas' direction. 'Since early this morning my sister and I have been
deafened by the most outrageous noise coming from the
other side of the house. What it must be like for the guests
on that side I shudder to think. Workmen everywhere,
far more than there has been up till now. One cannot hear
oneself speak!'

Anna suppressed an impatient sigh. 'I'm sorry you
have been disturbed,' she apologised, 'but there was—a
nasty accident yesterday. My mother and little Martha
Warrender were trapped by a fall of stone.'

'I heard about that and I am sorry, but I don't think it
excuses the bedlam we have had to suffer this morning,'
the disgruntled lady pointed out. 'My sister takes a little
rest after her coffee break at eleven o'clock and today
that has been impossible. If you have men at work you
ought to control the noise they make as a concession to
your guests.'

'I did my best,' Anna said, 'but some officials from
Nicosia came to look at the excavations in case the
workmen have stumbled on something of archaeological
interest. There has certainly been a house of some kind
here in the past, or it could have been a seaside village.'

'Indeed?' Mrs Pope was vaguely interested. 'All the
same, I do have to lodge my complaint about the noise. It

is quite distressing, and I expect you to do something about it as quickly as possible.'

'Perhaps I can help.' Andreas had stepped forward with his most attractive smile. 'I suggest that you and your sister would be happier at the Crescent Beach for a few days until Miss Rossides has cleared up the problem of the extra workforce. Nothing more will be done with the excavations for the swimming-pool, I can assure you, but there could be some further digging to establish what has been found. I understand how you feel about the unexpected noise,' he added without a flicker of derision, 'and I think you would be more comfortable at the Crescent Beach.'

'But it's a four-star hotel!' Mrs Pope protested. 'In no way could my sister and I afford the extra cost.'

'It would not be expected of you,' he told her pleasantly. 'Shall we just say it is all part of the service? In Cyprus we hope that our guests will enjoy every minute of their stay with us.'

Mrs Pope hesitated. 'Does that mean the Crescent Beach and the Villa Severus are one and the same hotel?' she enquired.

'No—we are quite separate,' Anna put in.

'But we aim to please.' Andreas was still smiling, waiting for the decision he expected Mrs Pope to make. 'There will be no inconvenience as far as you and your sister are concerned,' he promised. 'A maid from the Crescent Beach will come to pack for you and your luggage will be in your room whenever you care to come across.'

The generous arrangements began to appeal to Mrs Pope, but there were some questions still to be asked.

'We have one full week of our holiday still to take,' she informed him. 'I would not wish to undertake a second removal in a day or two.'

'That will not be necessary. You will remain at the Crescent Beach, on full board, until you leave the island.'

Placated, at last, the lady nodded her agreement.

'If you can assure me that my sister will not be unduly disturbed,' she allowed, 'we will accept your offer. I must say it is more than generous.'

'It is a pleasure,' Andreas assured her, tongue in cheek. 'I hope you will be happy at the Crescent Beach for the remainder of your holiday.'

Mrs Pope turned away, completely amazed by her success.

'Andreas, you hypocrite!' Anna laughed under her breath. 'Talk about a golden tongue! But you were always like that. I remember how you charmed everybody if you wanted something badly enough!'

'I wanted that dreadful woman off your back,' he said. 'I know her type. She would have used her dissatisfaction like the Sword of Damocles for the rest of her stay and you have more to do than pander to her whims.'

'You were magnificent.' She was still laughing. 'I couldn't believe the change in her expression when you told her she would be living four-star at no extra cost for the remainder of her holiday. You were brilliant about Cyprus, too, and the way we like to treat our guests.'

'I meant that bit,' he said, taking her arm. 'We have a lot of lee-way to make up on this island and I like to think I could be part of it. We can't afford too many Mrs Popes if we want to be considered an ideal holiday resort. I know you've grasped all that, but sometimes it can be difficult.'

'What will Lara say?' she asked. 'You seem to have taken the law into your own hands.'

'I'm managing the Crescent Beach,' he told her. 'Lara can't object when she taught me all I know, and I think she would have dealt with your problem in the same way.'

'Only if the villa was part of her empire!' Anna was the efficient hotel proprietress again. 'You must let me share the cost—recompense you in some way,' she insisted 'After all, you are full board over there and Mrs Pope and her sister are only half-board.'

'I've done my arithmetic,' he said with a slow smile. 'It will be well worth the extra cash.'

'It isn't business,' she pointed out.

'Perhaps not.' He led her towards the office door. 'I'll pick you up at three o'clock for the hospital.'

She was ready at three, waiting in the hall when he arrived in the big white Mercedes she had noticed once or twice before in the grounds of the Crescent Beach.

'It's Lara's car,' he explained. 'She's going to be busy in the hotel all afternoon. Tomorrow she hopes to take Marty to visit your mother.'

'Mama will enjoy that. She's very fond of Martha.'

'We all are,' he said, helping her into the front passenger seat. 'She is an exceptional child.'

They made the short distance to the hospital in record time.

'This is slightly different to the pick-up,' Anna observed. 'I feel quite regal!'

'Lara bought it a few days ago in Nicosia,' he explained. 'She likes a roomy car and she will need it in the mountains.'

'Have you settled on a villa yet?' The question was almost forced from her as she thought of them together.

'I haven't settled anything,' he said as he negotiated a busy crossing. 'It will be entirely Lara's decision. She wants something apart—something away from the holiday crowds, preferably outside a village. Nikos might be helpful in that respect,' he decided. 'He knows the Troodos very well.'

'But so do you,' she reminded him. 'Years ago they were practically our second home.'

She had not meant to bring up the happier past when they had skied at Plantres and explored the high mountain passes around St Hilarion rising far below. She had not meant to recall the past at all in case he might think her unduly sentimental or trying to assert some sort of claim on him now that he had returned to the land of his birth.

Her mother's small cubicle was surrounded by flowers, gifts sent in that morning by people who had heard of the accident at the villa, pink and red carnations, and yellow roses, and pale irises the colour of moonstones, and great spikes of gladioli, and stralytzia like flaming swords in the sun.

'I had no idea I had so many friends,' Dorothy smiled. 'Such beautiful flowers! They make me feel better already, although I'm trussed up like a chicken and mustn't laugh.' She looked beyond Anna to the man standing at the foot of her bed. 'I knew you would come, Andreas, and thank you for the fruit you sent. The peaches are delicious.'

'I remembered your preference,' he told her, moving to take her hand in his. 'Get well quickly, Mama!' he said. 'We're going to miss you.'

Anna pretended to study the cards on the flower arrangements, her eyes blurred by tears. If only everything had been the same, if they had been coming to her mother with mutual love in their hearts this would have been a happy reunion.

'I'm not going to be much use to Anna for a very long time,' Dorothy was saying. 'How stupid of me to fall down like that when she needs all the help she can get just now. It is our busiest time and even one pair of hands can make a difference.'

Andreas bent over the bed, taking her slender hands in his. 'You are to stop worrying,' he said firmly. 'Anna and I will manage quite well.'

'Does that mean you are going to stay on the island?' Dorothy's eyes were eager on his. 'Does it mean you will be here for a while, at least?'

'I'll be at the Crescent Beach,' he assured her, 'right next door. I've already told Anna that she can count on me for help or advice at any time. It might go against the grain at first,' he added with a brief smile, 'but I think she will come round to my way of thinking in the end.'

'It's such a relief,' Dorothy sighed, 'knowing you will

be there. The doctors are talking about a rest, about me going to the mountains for the summer, but I don't think I can do that.'

'Why not?' he demanded. 'We can fix something up in no time. You must stop arguing, Mama, and let us take care of you.' He smiled at her disarmingly. 'You wouldn't exactly be an asset at the villa just now, you know!'

'I don't want to be a burden and now you are making it impossible for me to refuse to go,' Dorothy declared. 'Perhaps I'll go for a week or two once I am sure that Anna can manage on her own,' she conceded.

There was a tap on the door behind them and Anna turned quickly to see Nikos' mother standing in the aperture, smiling in at them. Kiria Masistas was a small, dark woman with inquisitive black eyes like a bird's and a smooth, round face framed by abundant black hair with no suggestion of grey in it anywhere. As a country matron in mourning for her late father, she wore black, but with a stylishness which suggested that her clothes had come from one of the grander establishments in Nicosia if not from Athens itself. The cross carried on a chain round her neck was of heavy gold and she wore a gold bracelet on her left arm. Anna kissed her dutifully on both cheeks.

'How kind of you to come right away,' she said, relieving her mother's visitor of the large basket of fruit she carried. 'We have been so anxious, Kiria Masistas, but now it seems that Mama will get well quite quickly if she continues to rest as the doctors advise.'

Helena Masistas went straight to the bedside, acknowledging Andreas with a curt nod.

'Dorothy Rossides, what is this I find?' she demanded with kindly concern. 'You, of all people, in a hospital bed!'

'Helena,' Dorothy said, her sapphire eyes gleaming. 'I thought you would come without delay.'

'You knew I would come.' They kissed, friends of old standing although their circumstances were so different.

'Nikos has aquainted me with all the details including the fact that you saved the life of a child.'

'Nikos has exaggerated,' Dorothy assured her. 'We were too curious, Helena, wanting to see how the new swimming-pool was getting on—altogether too curious!'

Helena regarded her closely. 'Nikos was right,' she declared after the briefest of pauses. 'You are in need of a holiday when you are finally allowed out of here. You are in need of good mountain air, Dorothy Rossides, and we have plenty of that at Stroumbi. You will come straight to us from the hospital and Nikos will bring you.' She held up her hand to obstruct any argument that might be put forward. 'I will not hear of a refusal,' she announced, 'because it is already settled.'

Dorothy's eyes went beyond her. 'Andreas has come home,' she said, smiling in his direction. Helena kept her back turned.

'So I have heard.' Her lips were firmly compressed. 'I hope he will not cause you further heartache before he goes away again, as Nikos says he will.'

Anna's heart was racing, wanting to protest, wanting to deny what Nikos had said, but already Andreas was answering for her, politely but to the point.

'I will be here for some time, Kiria Masistas, doing all I can for Anna and her mother. I am working at the Crescent Beach next door to the villa and I have also bought some land on the other side.'

'Candy's Place,' Anna explained helpfully.

'I heard you were interested in buying land,' Helena acknowledged distantly. 'You have chosen wisely with all that frontage to the sea. What do you intend to make of it? Another luxury hotel?'

'I'm leaving it as it is at present,' Andreas told her smoothly. 'I'm not taking any chances when it could easily be part of new excavations on that side.'

'People are digging everywhere these days,' Helena sniffed. 'Even in the mountains we are afraid to open up more land in case we stumble upon an ancient city and

everything is taken over by the authorities, but at least
we have our orange groves and the vineyards and the
carob trees and plenty of good fresh air.' She turned to
Anna. 'You must keep in touch with us, my dear, and
whenever your mother can be moved you will bring her
to Stroumbi.'

'Helena, do you think it is wise for me to come straight
away?' Dorothy asked, looking over her friend's head to
where Andreas stood beside the door. 'Perhaps I should
go home for a while.'

'That is foolish,' Helena decided. 'In a few more weeks
the temperature on the coast will be unbearable and I
know how you will insist on working if you are still at the
villa. Come to the mountains and let Anna cope for a
while until she has changed her mind about coming to
Stroumbi permanently. That will make us happy, I can
assure you.' She smiled a little at a private thought. 'We
have always wanted her in the family and surely she will
see how right it is now.'

'You were ever a matchmaker, Helena!' Dorothy
laughed. 'You have not yet learned to let the young ones
decide for themselves.'

'Sometimes they do not know what is best for them.'
Helena cast another glance in Andreas' direction. 'They
are foolish or ambitious or too fond of their own way. I
can see no reason to let them spoil their lives for want of
some good advice.' She turned to go. 'But we have tired
you talking so much,' she acknowledged. 'Just remember
what I have said. You are to come to the mountains and
bring Anna with you.'

Andreas held the door open for her.

'Nikos will bring you some flowers in the morning,'
Helena said, bending to kiss Dorothy on the cheek.
'*Perastika*. I will come to visit you again quite soon.'

'*Kali andamossi*!' Anna said almost thankfully, seeing
the fatigue on her mother's face.

Dorothy closed her eyes as soon as Helena had gone.
'She means well,' she said, a note of apology in her voice

as she met Andreas' amused eyes. 'She has so much authority on the estate that she exercises it everywhere without thinking.'

'That was always her fault,' he answered lightly. 'I well remember her on the ski slopes telling everyone what to do till she had that accident herself.'

'And never skied again,' Anna remembered. 'You needn't go to Stroumbi, Mama, if you don't want to. We can arrange something else.'

'I would never hear the end of it if I didn't go,' Dorothy predicted. 'When Helena makes a gesture it is foolish to turn it down and she is really trying to be kind. She does want to help.'

'There will be time enough to make decisions when you are well enough,' Anna said, bending over the bed, 'and now you must rest and I'll come back in the morning.' She kissed her mother's cheek. 'They'll take good care of you here.'

Andreas came back to the bed. 'Sleep well, Mama,' he said. 'If you can have more than one visitor tomorrow Lara would like to bring Marty in just to say "Thank you".'

'I'd like that.' Dorothy stretched out her hand to him and he crushed her fingers in his. 'You will come too, perhaps?'

"Every day,' he promised, 'till you tell me not to!'

The sapphire-blue eyes were very bright as they looked back into his. 'That will never happen,' she said. 'Andreas, it's good to have you back.'

He held her hand for a moment longer. 'It's good to be back, Mama,' he said.

Anna walked ahead of him along the corridor. 'You've been forgiven,' she said under her breath. 'Mama could never hold a grudge for very long.'

'And you, Anna?' he asked, looking down at her as they reached the open air.

'I—it isn't important how I feel,' she said unsteadily. 'It was what she thought that mattered most, and what

she needs now is peace of mind and no more work about
the hotel. I'm going to make sure of that, at least.'

'By marrying Nikos?' he asked, his dark brows
suddenly drawn together in a frown. 'Is that the logical
solution to all your problems?'

A hot colour flew to her cheeks. 'You have no right to
ask that,' she retorted. 'None at all!'

'I have your interests at heart. We were brought up
together, remember.' He opened the car door for her. 'In
the ordinary way that should mean a lot.'

The surge of emotion she had tried to hold back could
no longer be restrained. 'It means nothing, surely,' she
declared without looking at him. 'I can't expect you to
feel—responsible for me, if that's what you are offering
to do.'

'It wasn't, as a matter of fact,' he said, getting in
behind the wheel. 'I just want to make sure you're not
making a terrible mistake.'

'By marrying someone who wants me—someone who
is kind and considerate and wouldn't hurt me in any
way?' She looked straight ahead as they turned into the
busy street. 'Someone I could rely on who would always
be there when I needed him.'

He considered her brief summing up of happiness for a
full minute before he said, 'That seems to describe Nikos
admirably, but it doesn't sound very much like you. I
can't imagine you playing tennis and picking oranges for
the rest of your life, and I can't see you being content with
a doormat. Besides which, you would be under Kyria
Masistas' broad little thumb in next to no time, with all
the spirit crushed out of you as effectively as she crushes
the oranges in that great press of hers up there on the
estate. It used to fascinate me as a kid—all the pith and
juice running out and the rest thrown away. Do you
remember how much in awe of her we were in those
days?'

'I've stopped remembering,' Anna said, her heart too
full of memories to answer him truthfully. 'Everything

has changed, everything that used to matter.'

'I'm sorry about that,' he returned briskly. 'I would have had it otherwise.'

They drove in comparative silence along the waterfront where the golden balls of spent mimosa had been blown from the trees, making a yellow carpet on the ground. There was something sad about that, she thought, all the beauty of spring shed so quickly to be trampled thoughtlessly underfoot or swept away beyond recall. The trees were still green, their leaves stirring in the wind, but some of the magic had gone and when she looked out across the bay it was ruffled by the afternoon wind which blew in so determinedly across the sand, a strong and ruthless wind with no thought of the damage it might do, although its breath was warm.

When they reached the Crescent Beach she said she could easily walk the short distance to the villa on her own.

'I'll go along the shore,' she said. 'It will give me a breath of sea air.'

'I'll walk with you.'

'No, please don't; you have done enough. Thank you for taking me to the hospital, Andreas. It was certainly a help.'

Dismissed, he let her go, watching as she crossed the terraces to the beach where the waves pounded against the stone breakwater like the fury in his own heart.

She did not see him again for a few days, although she knew that he had visited her mother at the hospital each afternoon, taking Lara and Martha with him on the first occasion and bringing books and magazines for her mother to read. He knew that she would visit in the morning so perhaps he was avoiding her or was busy with Lara and the affairs of the Crescent Beach.

When he finally came to the villa he had something to show her.

'Take a look at these,' he said, holding out several

ancient coins. 'They were found on your site. Interesting, eh?'

Their hands touched as she picked up one of the coins, studying it carefully before she could trust herself to speak. She knew enough to place it as a silver gros of the Frankish period, recognising the cross and the king's portrait on the obverse with orb and sceptre, but which king?

'Hugh IV or Peter II, the experts say,' he informed her.

'Are there many?' She passed the coin back to him without touching his hand.

'Quite a few, and they hope to find more, of course. They're digging in Candy's Place now. Apparently this was a villa belonging to the Lusignans, or some branch of the family, but most of the buildings were to the east of your site.'

'Under Candy's Place?'

He nodded. 'There's evidence of quite a large establishment, walls and foundations going farther back than the sixteenth century even—perhaps to Byzantine times. There's a double-headed eagle with a sword and orb in its claws carved on one of the stones they've excavated. Everything's happening with tremendous speed since you started to scoop out your swimming-pool,' he added reflectively.

'I'm sorry, Andreas,' she said. 'It might upset all your plans for another grand hotel.'

He smiled. 'You have a fixation about my future plans,' he said briefly, 'but they are not so grand, Anna. I want to keep this shoreline as it has always been—as we remember it—and Lara agrees with me. We can make Candy's Place the "in thing" without spoiling the atmosphere and we can have a "dig" into the bargain. It's called making the most of adversity, I guess. We can make old King Peter or Hugh or whoever he was work for us in a lot of ways provided they don't unearth a palace or something equally inconvenient.'

'Which means you won't be able to do anything about

Candy's Place for some time yet,' she guessed.

'I can't add to it, if that's what you mean, but I can keep the present buildings intact. We'll still be neighbours, Anna, and I think we ought to work together. I don't intend to build anything more sinister than a breakwater, and that could benefit you, too.'

'We seem to be both in the same sort of situation,' she admitted, 'waiting for official sanction to go ahead with our plans, but it can't matter so much to you. Will you be here all summer if you mean to build your breakwater at Candy's Place?'

If there had been anticipation in her voice she had tried to hide it, telling herself that it could not really matter, one way or another, whether he stayed or not.

'Off and on,' he said. 'I'm furnishing the flat at Paphos and Lara has made a final decision about the villa in the Marathasa. She has found just what she wanted, at last.'

'She—must be very happy.' Her voice had sounded tense and strained.

'She has been planning this for a long time.' He put the coins back into his pocket 'She will go to Rome and bring Philip back with her when everything is ready.'

'Philip?'

'Her husband. Marty's father.'

Shock was Anna's first reaction, although she had thought about Lara's husband several times during the past few days, imagining him dead, or neglectful or just too busy to accompany his attractive wife when she travelled so far afield in pursuit of her own career. Andreas had referred to her very much as the power behind the throne and she certainly seemed a model of proficiency when it came to management, but now Philip Warrender was coming to Cyprus to settle at the villa Lara had found for them in the Marathasa, a mountain retreat that they may have planned for a very long time.

She looked up at Andreas, at last, seeing the futile anger in his dark face and the hidden pain in his eyes. It

mattered to him that Philip Warrender was on his way to
the Marathasa; it mattered to him very much. Her heart
contracted with its own pain, but she knew that he would
not tolerate her sympathy.

'We are good friends,' he said pointedly. 'Philip and
Lara have done a lot for me. When I first went to work
for them I knew very little about the hotel trade, but they
were patient because they knew I had this desire to
succeed—Lara calls it my potential—and they were
willing to take a chance with me. That's why I could
never let them down.'

And so, in love with Lara almost inevitably, he had
made his decision not to let anyone down. Perhaps he
had come back to Cyprus in order to get away, but there
had been no escaping. Lara had followed in his wake and
now they were all together again—Philip and Andreas
and Lara, who was Philip's wife.

'I'm sure you won't,' Anna said automatically,
although only a few days ago she had accused him of
infidelity where his former family was concerned.
Perhaps it wasn't the same—young people had a right to
fly the nest—and this adult love of his would be
something more intense, somthing so soul-destroying in
its hopelessness that it might finally consume him
altogether.

'Let me know what you decide about your mother,' he
said. 'I can easily pick her up at the hospital when she is
fit enough and bring her home.'

'No, Andreas!' Her voice faltered. 'I can't go on
accepting your help like this.' She spoke with her head
turned, ready to walk away. 'Nikos has offered to take
her to Stroumbi once she is fit enough to travel.'

'You'll go with her, of course?'

'I'll drive up with them, but I can't stay for more than a
few hours.' She was in command of her emotions now.
'You should recognise that. Hotels don't run by
themselves. It's a twenty-four-hours-a-day job.'

'I've offered to stand in for you,' he reminded her. 'I

know more about hotels than Nikos Masistas knows about oranges or olives and I have a right to help you, Anna. I owe it to your mother.'

She pushed the blown hair back from her forehead. Debts, she thought, everyone owing something to someone else, no matter how much it hurt.

'I don't think Mama looks at it that way.' She moved up the terrace steps. 'All she wanted was your affection.'

While I wanted your love, she said in her heart. I wanted it always!

A week later they were on their way to the mountains, Anna and her mother and Nikos, driving through the dappled sunlight along the coast road to Paphos and on to Stroumbi with the Troodos etched against a pale sky ahead of them and clad in pine and cypress and cedar in every shade of green.

Before they came to the village Nikos swung the car off the main road and soon they were climbing through one picturesque little settlement after another with the mountains crowding round them and vineyards everywhere. A wide expanse of hills and valleys stretched from the foot of the Troodos, cradling the rivers that flowed westward to the sea, but it was the peaks themselves which dominated the scene. High and fierce and seemingly impenetrable, with monastries and ruined castles crowning their incredible heights, it seemed impossible that anything could ever have been built there, but long ago men of faith had raised their churches and made their homes in that awesome wilderness of rock and stone and they had endured.

Nikos turned the car off the mountain road, winding down into a remote valley where orchards spread on either side of a broad stream and the farmhouse which was their destination lay quietly in the sun. It was a large, rambling house, old and weather-worn and shaded by tall eucalyptus trees and Cyprus pines growing strongly to shelter it in the north. It was many years since Anna had last been there, but nothing had changed The stillness

remained and a sense of peace was everywhere as they
drew up before the open main door to be greeted by Kiria
Masistas at her welcoming best.

'What a day you have for your journey,' she smiled.
'Not one cloud in sight.' She opened the door on
Dorothy's side of the car. 'Welcome to our home,' she
greeted her expected guest. 'You will recover well here
away from the rush and bustle of the coast.'

Anna helped her mother out while Nikos carried her
small suitcase into the hall.

'You have not come prepared to stay for long,' Helena
remarked at sight of such a modest amount of luggage.
'You will not be wise to return to the heat of Limassol
until you are fully recovered. I have a proposition to
make,' she added, glancing in Anna's direction. 'We
would gladly let you occupy the cottage for as long as you
wish. I have had it prepared for you especially, and
Thelma will look after your comfort and cook for you. Of
course, you will stay here, in our home, for as long as you
wish before you decide,' she added, ushering them into
the vast, dim hallway where three arches led to the
garden beyond. 'There is no hurry.'

Anna could see by her mother's expression that the
cottage in the grounds would be more to her liking
because it would give her independence of a kind and a
certain amount of privacy which she would not have in
the farmhouse itself, large though it was. Helena
entertained extensively during the summer months and
Nikos' friends were free to come and go as they pleased.
It was open house to all, as it had always been.

Helena hurried them up the shallow staircase to the
rooms she had prepared for them.

'You will stay over the weekend,' she said to Anna,
making it sound more like a command than an
invitation. 'Nikos will have arranged something for
tomorrow, I'm sure.'

'I wish I could,' Anna said, 'but I must go back to the
villa. I haven't a deputy, you see.' She thought about

Andreas and his offer to help, but she had effectively rebuffed him without actually knowing why. 'I'd love to stay, but I must get back by six o'clock—just in case anything has gone wrong.'

'Surely there is someone who could take your place for a day or two,' Helena suggested. 'It is a mistake to think you can't go off for an hour or two and leave your responsibilities to someone else.'

'I suppose so,' Anna agreed, 'but we haven't got such a big staff to fall back on. Andreas offered, but I—didn't think it was fair to ask him when he has so much to do looking after the Crescent Beach.'

Helena frowned. 'I hear he has done very well for himself,' she observed, 'buying one of the new flats at Paphos into the bargain. It rather looks as if he has decided to stay in the island. I wonder what his origins were.'

'His parents were very dear friends of mine,' Dorothy said quietly, 'and I'm glad Andreas has made good at something he appears to like. He was always very—alert.'

'Of course, you brought him up, I remember.' Helena opened the door of a large room at the head of the stairs where the shutters had been closed against the bright sunlight. 'I was surprised when he went off like that at a moment's notice, virtually without a word.'

Dorothy looked distressed. 'It is something I have forgotten,' she said. 'We must all make our peace with each other, sooner or later.'

'*I* would have remained affronted,' Helena decided. 'After all, you were his parents in everything but name. He was a strange youth, I remember, always wanting to be out in front, always succeeding where others failed. Nikos and he never really got on. Superficially it appeared that they were friends, but I sensed a rivalry between them even in those days.' She glanced at Anna once more. 'What do you think of the Returned Conqueror, my dear?'

Faced with the one question she was not prepared to answer, Anna crossed to the massive wardrobe which stood against one of the painted walls to hang up her mother's coat. 'I think he is still very ambitious,' she said without turning, 'but there is a virtue in that, too, and he still has many friends on the island.'

'And some new ones as well, I understand.' Helena was pulling out drawers, all beautifully lined with lavender paper. 'You will put your clothes in here, Dorothy, and then we must have something refreshing to drink. It is almost eleven and Kypros will be on the terrace as the clock strikes the hour. He is a monument of punctuality, as you know!'

She left them with an expansive smile. 'Come down as soon as you are ready,' she said.

'That means at once!' Anna said, looking across the room into her mother's anxious sapphire eyes. 'Are you going to be happy here?' she asked bluntly. 'If not, we can decide on the cottage right away.'

'The cottage will be a lovely bolt-hole,' Dorothy agreed, 'but I'll stay here for a day or two—perhaps even a week. They will be affronted otherwise.'

'It's an old-fashioned word, isn't it? Affronted. I thought it sounded a little bit prim.'

'Helena is prim, although she pretends to be sophisticated. She has a code of ethics which she hangs on to relentlessly and it sounds as if she would be most unforgiving if anyone went against her will.'

'Not like you!' Anna put her arm about her mother's shoulders. 'Promise me you won't stay here for a moment after you feel her welcome is cooling. You won't have any problems with Papa Masistas, I'm sure, but Nikos' mother will want to "manage" you from the word go.'

'I'm not easily managed when I don't want to be,' Dorothy protested with a return of her former spirit, 'so we'll keep the cottage in mind. It's on the far side of the estate, isn't it?'

'I think so. Anyway, we can soon find out,' Anna

promised, moving towards the door.

They retraced their steps to the floor below to find Nikos and his father waiting on the terrace. Kirie Masistas was a handsome man in his early fifties, big and strong, with the look of the open air about him and a mane of thick, dark hair to match the splendid moustache which adorned his upper lip. It had been trained to curl upwards at each end, giving his whole face an air of distinction, and two very dark eyes looked out at the world with a humour and tolerence which suggested infinite understanding. As soon as he saw his visitors a vast smile revealed two rows of splendid white teeth and he held out both hands in welcome.

'*Kherete!* We are pleased to see you here, at last, Dorothy Rossides,' he said. 'You will stay with us for as long as you please and we will soon restore the colour to your cheeks. Good air and good fresh fruit will soon put you right.' He kissed Dorothy on both cheeks. 'It is far too long since you were last with us.'

The warmth of his welcome was quite genuine and some of the tension was eased in Anna's heart before he turned to her to say, 'You must be a busy young woman when you have not had time to visit us for so long, but I hope you will come often now. We miss the girls, although they come home for their holidays, but the house is far too quiet nowadays.'

His twin daughters were in school in England, but Anna knew that they would return whenever they could because this was a close-knit household typical of the island and its long tradition of family unity and her mother would be safe under Kypros Masistas' roof.

Nikos was helping to carry out large jugs of freshly crushed orange and plates of sweetmeats.

'These used to be your favourites, if I remember rightly,' he said to Anna.

'Honey cakes,' she smiled. 'Home baked and utterly tempting!'

'Don't gorge yourself or you won't do justice to your

lunch,' he warned. 'The kitchens are a hive of industry with everyone trying their best to impress you.'

Anna glanced at her watch. 'I mustn't stay too long,' she said. 'I really must get back to the hotel.'

'Nikos will take you,' Helena said, passing the orange-juice she had measured into tall, frosted glasses for their refreshment. 'There is surely no need to rush off so quickly when we have seen so little of you these past two years.'

Dorothy sat down beside her host who immediately engaged her in animated conversation, mostly about the past, and gradually all the concern faded from her eyes. Kypros Masistas had a sense of humour to match her own and that in itself was encouraging. Anna began to feel glad that they had come.

While her mother was encouraged to rest in one of the cane reclining chairs under the vine pergola she went with Nikos to view the orange-grove, walking with him between the trees as she had done many years ago after the twins' birthday party in June.

'It's all exactly as I remember it,' she said. 'This lovely valley with the mountains so near and the scent of blossom everywhere. Will you stay here, Nikos, for the rest of your life?'

'Where else?' He had been brought up with a sense of belonging. 'I'm fourth generation Masistas and it's expected of me as an only son.'

'It's such a rewarding way of life,' she mused 'being part of something like this, being—sort of sure of your destiny, I suppose I mean. You couldn't possibly throw it away for something trivial.'

'When I was young I wanted to be a fisherman. You know—out in boats all the time, sailing everywhere, but a holiday on Crete cured me of all that.' He laughed, showing teeth as gleaming as his father's in an equally engaging smile. 'We were caught in a storm and I was terrified!'

'I thought you liked the sea!'

'I do, in a decent sized boat, but this was a very small caique which threatened to turn turtle miles from land and I didn't really enjoy getting wet with all my clothes on!' He put an arm round her waist, drawing her close. 'I think I feel safer on dry land. How about you?'

'Feeling safe?' She looked up at him. 'I—I'm grateful because my mother is with you and she will get well quickly here among the mountains. I feel that a great load has been lifted off my mind.'

'That wasn't what I meant,' he said. 'I wanted to know how you felt about being here all the time—about marrying me.' Suddenly he had taken her in his arms, kissing her with a passion she had not expected in him. 'There's no point in waiting, Anna. There's room for all of us up here and my family would make you welcome, you know that.'

Shaken, she tried to free herself from his embrace, aware of the heady scent of orange blossom all around them.

'Nikos, can we not talk about this just now?' she pleaded. 'I can't abandon everything at the villa just to feel "safe" here among the mountains and——'

'And you're not in love with me? Isn't that what you are trying to say, Anna, only you can't put it into words because you think it will hurt me? Well, it will, and I'm not going to let it happen,' he declared. 'I'm going to wait and wait till you change your mind and you can't stop me.'

'Oh, Nikos!' she said. 'Why is it all so hard? I like you—I always have—but loving is another thing—something very different. You come on it quite suddenly or you've known it all along, but either way everything is changed.'

He drew back, walking a little way ahead of her along the path between the orange trees, picking off a leaf here and there.

'You know a lot about it, Oh Worldly One!' he mocked. 'But what about if it doesn't work out for you?

What if you find that this perfect love of yours isn't all you expect and it lets you down in the end?'

'I would—have to have come to terms with that,' she said unsteadily. 'Perhaps I already have.'

'Is that a cue for me to wait, silently and patiently, till it is all over?'

She could have told him that it would never be over, that her first love was her love now and always would be, however forlorn, but she had hurt him enough.

'It's time we went back,' she said, turning in the direction of the white farmhouse gleaming through the trees. 'I'm sorry, Nikos.'

'Don't apologise.' He took her arm. 'We'll start again where we left off, but just remember if you are knocked out by the little blind god you can always come to me and I'll gather up the pieces with sympathy and understanding any time.'

'You will probably change your mind long before then.' She tried to smile. 'Someone else will come along.'

'Not for me.' There was an odd conviction in his voice, 'I know what I want, Anna, and I've never been keen on second best. Never been used to it,' he mused,

Which was true, Anna thought ruefully. He was an only son who had seldom been denied anything within reason by loving parents who thought only of his happiness and he had accepted that all his wishes would be granted until now.

'I'm sorry,' she said again. 'I didn't mean to hurt you, Nikos.'

'We'll forget about it,' he said in a voice so hurt that he might as well have admitted it. 'I'll take you back to Limassol after lunch.'

The meal they shared at a table set out on the terrace was an excellent one, There were several kinds of salads and cold meats to suit every taste, and small, sweet cakes served afterwards with their coffee which they drank under the canopy of vines. Kypros Masistas sat well back in his chair, splendidly replete, his smiling eyes embracing everybody.

'This is how it should be,' he declared. 'A full house and a happy one,' He lit a large cigar, tweaked his moustache upwards at both ends, and lay back to contemplate the view they had down the silent valley. Most of what he saw was his. 'The land is a great satisfaction, Dorothy,' he continued. 'It gives back all a man puts into it and more. I've developed this valley since I took over from my father ten years ago, but even before that I was thinking about trees. Now you will see that the whole hillside is planted and one day Nikos will plant again.' He looked proudly at his son. 'I hope nothing will prevent that,' he added fervently. 'No rushing off after false gods. Soon I hope to see him married and settled down in the place where he was born. We have no wish to hurry him, you understand, but if he brings the right girl to the valley we will be greatly relieved.' Looking across the terrace at Anna, he added deliberately, 'Helena thinks he has already found her.'

There was nothing obtuse about this gallant old man; he said exactly what he felt without hesitation, expecting others to do the same. Helena's agile brain worked in a different way with much the same result.

'You must play more tennis, Anna,' she suggested. 'It is not good to be always cooped up indoors, working all day long. We have two courts here, out of use most of the time since I no longer play, and Nikos could easily bring you up for a game. It is not far to come and it will soon be too uncomfortable to play on the coast—so hot and sticky in the summer—but here, in the mountains, it is always cool.'

'It's quite a long drive,' Anna said, 'but thank you for inviting me. I could come in the pick-up if we are not too busy, although there are tennis courts at the Crescent Beach next door.'

'Nikos goes there often in his spare time,' Helena acknowledged, a hint of suspicion in her voice, 'but you will want to visit your mother, also.'

'I'll see that she gets here,' Nikos said as Anna got reluctantly to her feet.

Their goodbyes were said on the terrace with the sleeping house behind them. It was three o'clock and time for her mother's afternoon rest.

'We'll go back by Cedar Valley,' Nikos suggested as soon as they had left the narrow farm track behind. 'There is no great hurry and I haven't had you to myself for five minutes.'

'Half-an-hour,' Anna laughed, remembering their walk in the orange grove. 'You *do* exaggerate.'

He turned the car along the mountain road. 'It's a longer way round,' he admitted, 'but once we get to Kykko we'll be off the dust roads and into civilisation again.'

They went down into the beautiful Cedar Valley and up again by the breathtaking switchback road Anna remembered so well. Craggy peaks and lonely, isolated monasteries dominated their view as they wound through the Marathasa so that it was like a journey into the past as far as she was concerned, and Nikos, too, seemed to be silenced by so much grandeur, although he lived and worked among it. There was very little traffic on the road at that time of day, but before they reached the junction, with the Kykko monastry nestling on the mountainside above them, a car came towards them from the direction of Pedhoulas. It was a large car, taking up more of its share of the narrow dirt road they had followed for the past half-hour and Nikos pulled into a convenient passing place.

The car came on, slowly and carefully, the woman driver seemingly unsure of the sudden change of road surface, but it was a big and powerful car which should have given her no trouble at all, a white Mercedes in pristine condition with the sun visors down to protect the eyes.

Anna knew who it was before the two cars drew level.

Lara was at the wheel, her gaze fixed on the road ahead, while beside her sat a distinguished-looking man in a pale grey suit, his grey hair uncovered, his eyes hidden behind heavy, dark glasses as if the glare of the afternoon sun disturbed him. In the back of the car Martha and Susan sat studying a book, too absorbed by what they were reading to look up at passing strangers.

'Did you see who that was?' Nikos asked, watching the Mercedes through his wing mirror as it drew away. 'It was Lara driving with Martha and Susan in the back seat, I wonder who the man in front was.'

'Her husband.' Anna had controlled her voice with an effort.

'Husband?' Nikos queried, surprised. 'The general opinion was that she was a widow.'

'Opinions can be wrong. Lara has brought him here for some reason best known to herself.'

'Where from?'

'Rome.'

'I suppose Andreas knows all about it.'

'Yes, I think so.'

He considered the position carefully before he said, 'This will put his nose out of joint. They were always in each other's company, doing everything together.'

Anna continued to gaze through the windscreen. 'They worked together,' she said. 'Lara and her husband taught Andreas all he knows about the hotel trade and he is grateful, I suppose.'

'But he didn't expect to fall in love with the boss,' Nikos suggested. 'It happens often enough, you know, even in the best regulated businesses and the hotel trade is no exception. On the contrary, it would appear to lend itself to that sort of thing, if you ask me.' When she didn't answer him he added with slow deliberation, 'I suspected something of the kind from the very beginning, especially when he was so attentive where Martha was concerned. It's a sure road to a woman's heart, and you can see the child means a great deal to her. Martha is probably the only one.'

'That must make her doubly precious to Lara and her husband,' Anna pointed out, not wanting to prolong the conjecture about the occupants of the Mercedes which had now disappeared along the mountain road in a rising cloud of dust. Nikos, however, seemed obsessed by Andreas' reaction to what he considered a complicated situation all round.

'Do you think there might be a divorce in the offing?' he queried. 'All three of them just waiting for the law to take its course?'

Anna's heart seemed to miss a beat. 'We have no right to go on guessing,' she said. 'If Andreas and Lara are fond of each other our curiosity won't help at all. It's a dreadful situation to know that you are in love and everything has gone wrong for you.'

They had reached Pedhoulas where a carpet of fallen petals lined the narrow streets and the scent of cherry blossom hung in the windless air. In less than a month the cherries would be ripe in the orchards and on the garden trees of the lovely villas dotting the hillsides as far as the eye could see. It would be summer in its fullest grandeur with nature offering all she had to give.

'Do you want to go on to Moutoullas?' Nikos asked. 'There's plenty of time and I dare say Lara has found her ideal villa near there.'

Anna shook her head. 'I'd like to go straight home,' she said. 'It's almost five o'clock.'

The road continued to climb through the pine forests and finally they reached Podhromos, overflowing with early visitors and offering a splendid panorama over the slopes of the Troodos with the craggy summit of Olympus already casting its shadow on the valley below. All along the road to Troodos itself the hillsides were dotted with luxurious villas and little homesteads basking in the sunshine, and it was here that Anna imagined Lara had bought her new home. Within thirty miles of Limassol where her main interests lay, it would prove the ideal

retreat during the heat of the summer months, affording
her easy access in winter, too, when the high mountain
passes were covered in snow.

By the time they reached Limassol the sun was already
sinking towards the western horizon and the sky had
darkened in the east, showing a first sprinkling of stars.

'You'll stay for a meal?' she asked Nikos automatically. 'I'll put it on early for you.'

She had no idea that Andreas would be at the villa and
when she saw him she felt the colour rising in her cheeks.
'Don't tell me there's been a crisis.' she said jokingly.
'I've been away for all of eight hours.'

'Not unless you call Mrs Pope a crisis,' he smiled. 'She
wanted to know where you were so that she could pay you
for some extras that should have been on her bill, but I
told her she could contact you first thing in the morning if
she considered it urgent.' He looked beyond her to where
Nikos was talking to Paris. 'Had a good day in the
mountains?' he asked.

'Splendid,' she assured him. 'It makes you feel
refreshed and Mama is nicely settled in. Kirie Masistas is
wonderful company and they have known each other for
a very long time.'

'And Kiria Masistas?' he enquired,

'She'll be kind, too,' Anna predicted. 'For a while,
anyway, but the good news is that they have offered us
the use of a cottage on the estate with someone to cook
and clean for us whenever we decide to go.'

'And will you?'

'I think so—eventually. It will make us feel more
independent.'

'Is that important in the circumstances?'

'I think it is.' She took off her linen jacket, preparing to
go into the office. 'Andreas,' she added carefully, 'we met
Lara on the Pedhoulas road just before we came to the
junction. She was with Martha and Susan and, I think,
her husband.'

He did not seem to be surprised. 'They would be going

to Panayia, to the monastery. Philip was there for a spell three years ago and fell in love with the mountains then. I think the solitude helped him to look at the future in a different light.' His eyes seemed to darken at a memory. 'They may stay there for a day or two, although what Susan will think of monastic life remains to be seen. Did Lara send any message?' he asked abruptly. 'About the Crescent Beach,' he added as Nikos came across the hall to join them.

'We didn't stop.' Anna stood looking back at him from the doorway. 'Martha and Susan were engrossed in a book and Lara had to concentrate on her driving. The sun was in her eyes.'

'Perhaps we should have stopped,' Nikos mused, 'just to say "hullo", but I suppose we will meet them again quite soon.'

'Yes,' Andreas agreed abstractedly, 'I suppose you will.'

He walked away in the direction of the terraces towards the wall which separated the two hotels, his hands thrust deep in the pockets of his trousers, the dark and brooding look still in his eyes.

'A man with a load of trouble on his mind,' Nikos said in a speculative tone. 'It must be Lara. Who else could it be?'

'I'm not his confidante,' Anna said harshly. 'The days for that are long past. Andreas has grown away from us. Six years is a long time.'

He put his arm about her waist. 'Too long,' he said, 'if you ask me.'

CHAPTER SIX

SEVERAL days passed before they saw Andreas again, busy days because the swimming-pool excavations had become a focal point of local interest and several finds were made, suggesting that the Villa Severus had indeed been built on the site of an older villa long since buried in the sand which edged the Mediterranian Sea. The coins which Andreas had picked up on that first day could have been a cache of some sort, but later other coins had been discovered, together with a floor mosaic of Ganymede being carried off by the eagle of Zeus which was in almost perfect condition, proving that a second villa had stood beside the sea in the vicinity of Candy's Place.

All those years ago, Anna thought, people had lived and loved and died here, all with their various problems, as they were living now. Lovers had come and gone, empires had risen and passed away and Cyprus had been conquered and overthrown many times by Roman legions from the west and Turkish and Muslim invaders from the east.

When she had a moment to spare she walked along the edge of the excavations, aware that Candy's Place was now the main focus of attention. Inroads had already been made on the orchard area where Candy had kept his fishing gear. Whatever plans Andreas had made for the old man's tumbledown dwelling would now be suspended till the official decisions were taken, and she wondered if he was now regretting his eagerness to purchase it.

Turning back towards her own home she saw him coming towards her. 'Found anything?' he asked lightly.

'No. Why?'

'Everyone else has.' He stood contemplating the latest dig. 'I'm amazed at the amount of unimportant artefacts that have been lying right under Candy's nose for half a century without him realising the fact or even caring about who had been there before he decided to squat at this end of the bay. The other day I came across some "lead weights" he had been using on his fishing nets and they were all bronze follis of Heraclius which ought to have been in a museum long ago.'

'This is going to make a tremendous difference to Candy's Place,' she said with genuine sympathy. 'You won't be able to build on it as you like. It looks as if you have inherited all my problems in that respect.'

He sat down on the stone wall Candy had built to make an untidy little harbour before his property.

'My shoulders are broad enough,' he said philosophically. 'I don't suppose you will believe this, but I had no intention of making a killing over my deal with Candy. Of course,' he added drily, 'I had ideas for the future, but these may have to be curtailed now.' He glanced at her sideways. 'It may not be far off the mark to say that some of my plans will have to go by the board, but I am resilient in that respect, as you may have guessed. I've come to the conclusion that an ancient site is almost as good a proposition as a modern hotel in terms of the tourist trade. What could be more attractive than an active dig right on our doorstep, I ask you?'

She hadn't considered that.

'It would be on your property,' she reminded him.

'And partly on yours. You may have lost a swimming-pool, but you could have gained much more.'

'The two properties are quite separate.'

'Not any more. The excavations, however small and unimportant, will inevitably draw them together. One couldn't stand up without the other. It was a continuous garden, Anna, and, besides, I think I may have a tomb on my premises.' His tone was deliberately light. 'They dug out a section of it yesterday, so if we haven't exactly got a basilica on our hands at least we might have something of interest to show the public. The tomb was empty, by the way, so it was probably pillaged by some ancient relative of Candy who stumbled on it unaware.'

'You're making it sound very trivial,' she admonished, 'when it could be quite important.'

'I don't think so,' he said. 'The authorities don't seem impressed, but it could be important to you and me.'

She looked round at him in surprise. 'What do you mean?' she asked.

'We could develop Candy's Place together.'

She drew back from the suggestion. 'How could we?' she asked, 'Lara is already your partner.'

He shrugged. 'Lara would understand, She knew what I wanted to do at Candy's Place and this could be a bonus.'

'I don't know.'

'Think about it,' he said. 'I'm not going to involve Lara, or Philip, for that matter, because I'm not in their class, but I've learned a lot from them about how to go about this sort of thing. Philip is one of the most powerful property dealers in the West and I value his advice, but I could never compete with him.'

Except for Lara's affection, Anna thought painfully. Oh, Andreas, if it hadn't been for that I might have been glad to share Candy's Place with you, to develop it into something which would do credit to us both!

'I've told you that I want to see the villa as it is now—as it has always been,' he said, 'for your mother's sake, but perhaps there's a selfish motive behind that, too. All the time I've been away, all these years while I've been learning how to fend for myself, I've thought about it steeped in sunshine most of the time, like it has been since it was first built. Candy's Place came afterwards, remember, but that never seemed to matter very much because we all accepted Candy and we lived together in harmony. It was an ideal situation to grow up in.' He drew in a deep breath of the keen, fresh air. 'I used to think of it in London and New York when my horizon was bounded by skyscrapers, and I always promised myself that I would return. I know I could have persisted and written more often, but I was always too proud, or too foolish, to do that. I've explained all this to your mother,' he added abruptly, 'and now I'm telling you in case you can bring yourself to believe me.'

She held her breath, her strong white teeth fastening

on her lower lip for a moment before she said, 'I do believe you, although it can't make a lot of difference now. We've—grown away from each other, Andreas.' With an effort she kept her voice quite steady. 'It's no longer the same for either of us.'

He thought about her statement for a moment or two, frowning. 'You've changed a lot,' he admitted. 'Could it be the process of growing up, do you think?'

'We all change.' Her voice was steadier now. 'It's almost inevitable.'

'But not quite.' He looked at her fully, his eyes suddenly compelling. 'Are we partners as far as Candy's Place is concerned?'

'We may have no choice if they decide to extend the dig, she said'. 'In that case I couldn't very well argue.'

'Which isn't what I would call a convincing answer,' he said, 'but it will have to do for the present. When did you last visit your mother?'

'I've phoned every day, but I haven't been able to get up to Stroumbi again.' They turned away from the new excavations towards the beach. 'She seems to have settled down very well and the Masistas' are kindness itself, apparently.'

'I'm sure.' He strode across the sand beside her. 'I'm going up there—to Pedhoulas. Would you like to come?'

'It would be out of your way to take me to the Masistas'.'

'Not too far out of my way,' he decided. 'Twenty miles or so. Think about it and let me know.'

Before he could turn away she had made up her mind. It would be a journey into the past for both of them, but she had already gone down that road many times since his return. Once more could make little difference and her mother must want to see her.'

'I'd like to go, Andreas,' she said. 'Only I'd have to know that everything was running smoothly here before I took a whole day off.'

His eyes gleamed with amusement. 'When are you

going to realise that an hotel—even a small hotel—can run quite smoothly on its own for twenty-four hours or more if you have an efficient staff?' he demanded. 'Paris and Elli are quite competent and Francis runs his kitchens admirably without your supervision, I'm sure. We'll make it Friday, when your mid-week arrivals should have settled in and the Saturday rush hasn't begun.'

'If that will suit you.'

He shrugged. 'The Crescent Beach runs by itself. I'm only a cog.'

She laughed. 'A very important cog. You're managing the place.'

'That's what I'm trying to say. You manage by delegating. You can't be breathing down their necks all the time or they would never gain the experience they need.' He turned when they came to the wall. 'I have some papers for Lara to sign so I'll phone her in the morning.' he said. 'She has asked me to bring you several times.'

'Oh, but——'

Her protest was lost as he vaulted over the low wall. 'See you Friday,' he said. 'About ten o'clock.'

She hadn't counted on going to Lara's new home, especially with Andreas, but what reason could she possibly give for refusing now that she had accepted his offer? Her heart beat heavily for a moment and then she shrugged her despair aside. Why not? It would be stealing a day from the future, one day out of all the years ahead. She thought about the mountains and how often they had gone there in the past, golden days spent in the sun with the great peaks of the Troodos reaching up to a cloudless sky and a soft wind blowing across the valley floor. Such days had been perfection and this one day stolen from the future could be no less. Her heart lifted in sudden, inexplicable ecstasy as she walked along the terrace in front of the open loggia where most of her guests gathered for tea. As Andreas had just pointed out, it would be a day off and she had quite an efficient staff.

Friday seemed a long way away, but she had plenty to do. She would leave all the marketing to Francis because he went in early anyway to choose the fruit, and Elli and Paris could see to the other details between them.

Nikos had not been at the Crescent Beach all week so she concluded that he was too busy on the estate to come so far for a game of tennis, and when she phoned her mother Dorothy said vaguely that they were 'doing something with the vines'. She was almost childishly glad at the prospect of their meeting.

'I wondered if Andreas would offer to bring you,' she said. 'He is so busy these days.'

'Apparently not on a Friday.' Anna's heart was suddenly light. 'It's a good day for leaving hotel responsibilities behind, I gather.'

'When will you arrive?' The voice at the far end of the line was eager. 'Will you leave early?'

Anna hesitated. 'We're going to Pedhoulas first,' she explained. 'Andreas has to go to Lara's new villa for some sort of consultation, I gather, and to deliver some papers. I told you we passed Lara's car on the way home last week. She was with her husband—and Martha.'

'She may ask you to stay for lunch.' Dorothy sounded disappointed.

'I don't think she will, and Andreas knows I'm coming up principally to be with you for as long as possible. Will you tell Kiria Masistas and ask if it will be all right for me to come?'

'You don't need to ask,' Dorothy assured her. 'She is very fond of you, Anna, and so is Kypros. Do you know, he keeps me amused all day. He has a great fund of stories to tell and he seems to enjoy my company when Nikos is here to supervise the work.'

'I'm glad you're so well settled—and obviously so happy,' Anna said. 'Keep it up till Friday.'

At ten o'clock precisely Andreas arrived at the front door, driving his own car.

'All set?' he asked when she hurried across the hall to meet him. 'This all your luggage?' He glanced down at the suitcase and large basket she had placed near the door. 'It looks as if you're going for a week.'

'I'm taking some extra clothes for Mama,' she explained, 'and a few goodies for the family—fruit they don't grow and that sort of thing. Will it go in the back seat?'

"Easily.' He lifted suitcase and basket, casting a critical eye over the hall. 'Everything in order?'

'Absolutely. I'm looking forward to this, Andreas, and I'm not going to give the Villa Severus a single thought till we're on our way back.'

He held the front passenger door open for her after stowing her luggage in the back seat where she noticed a large bouquet of flowers encased in protective cellophane which was probably a gift for Lara.

'I ordered them from Limassol yesterday and they arrived just in time half-an-hour ago,' he said, getting in behind the wheel. 'I thought your mother would like them.'

'She'll be enchanted.' So, they were not a love-gift for Lara, after all. 'You know how fond she is of carnations.'

Paris saw them off, standing at the open door with an expression of great importance on his face, his white shirt tucked neatly into pale grey trousers, his bow tie of office immaculate. He had subdued his unruly curls with a side parting and much water, and his hands were folded discreetly behind his back.

'We've made his day.' Andreas laughed. 'What did I tell you about delegating responsibility? Paris will do you proud.'

They took the Troodos road out of Limassol, driving with the sun ahead of them as it came up over the mountains and filtered through the valleys. It was an ideal day with not a cloud in sight, a day like those she had remembered, and it seemed inevitable that Andreas should be by her side. Once or twice, glancing at his stern profile etched against the backdrop of hills on the far side of the car, it seemed as if they might regain the simple intimacy of a past long since gone, and she had to steel herself against remembering too vividly because everywhere she looked, to right or left, was heartbreakingly familiar. It was the road they had travelled so often, passing through the little villages they knew until they came close to the heart of the great peaks and the summer resorts built high on their craggy sides or sheltering in their shaded valleys. Mount Olympus shimmered in the sun, dedicated to Aphrodite long ago, and all the legendary nightingales of Plátres seemed to be singing in her ears.

Monasteries and ancient churches, waterfalls and deep-hidden gorges came and went with the road climbing among pines and plane trees one minute and plunging deep into a valley the next.

'We'll stop for coffee at the next taverna,' Andreas suggested. 'I don't think we're expected at the villa much before twelve o'clock. Let's make it somewhere we know,' he added. 'Papasolomontos', perhaps.'

He swung into a side road, bumping to a halt before the open frontage of a small restaurant where the stout proprietor was sitting at a table under a vine pergola smoking a contented pipe with half-a-dozen cronies who had gathered to hear his view on everything from the latest political situation to the state of the local vegetable crops. Peter Papasolomontos recognised them immediately.

'*Kherete!* I heard you had returned.' he said to Andreas in his native tongue, 'and you have not changed your girlfriend, either! That is good,' he declared. 'That is very good.'

Anna sat down on a red plastic chair, thinking how much nicer it would have been if Peter's old wicker chairs had survived. The old man's sense of hospitality had not altered, however. He brought thick, black Turkish coffee in little porcelain cups, placing a tray of sweetmeats beside them as a matter of course. Andreas asked about his family.

'They are well. We have five grandchildren now and Mama has come to stay with us since Papa died. You see,' he laughed, 'our family grows larger every year and we grow more and more content!'

Anna sipped the thick, harsh coffee politely, although she had never acquired a taste for it, and Andreas watched her effort with a smile.

'None of your instant stuff,' he pointed out. 'Thick and black and strong, as I remember it.'

'You always took water with it!' she condemned him. 'And mostly you preferred orange-juice.'

'Your father used to say that orange-juice was a woman's drink,' he reflected, 'and it took a man to appreciate Turkish coffee as it should be served.'

It was the first time he had mentioned her father without reserve and she wondered if he had decided to forget the past completely. It might no longer interest him now that he had a splendid new future ahead of him, a future of Lara's making, it seemed, blotting out the rancour of the past.

When they rose to go Peter Papasolomontos pressed a small parcel into her hands. 'For your Mama,' he said with a broad smile. 'For Kiria Rossides, whom I remember well.'

Anna knew that it would be the brand of Turkish Delight most popular in the small tavernas, the 'real thing', as her mother called it.

'We're going to see her this afternoon,' she said. 'I'm sure she will want me to thank you, Peter.'

'Kali andamossi!' Peter said. 'Come again.'

They reached Troodos at mid-day, climbing through the pine forests by the mountain road to Prodhromos with its summer hotels and flats and well-watered gardens basking in the sunshine. Andreas took a secondary road out of the resort where the houses thinned to a selected few, large villas and small, each with a spectacular view and hidden in their own bower of greenery to give them the measure of privacy they evidently desired.

'I think it might have been better if we had gone straight to the farm,' Anna said nervously. 'I feel like an intruder.'

'You had a perfectly legitimate invitation.' He turned to look at her. 'Lara knows that we will be going on to visit your mother and this is purely business. I have these papers for her to sign and she would have had to come to Limassol if I hadn't made the journey.'

He slowed the car as they came to a high white wall trailing hibiscus and bougainvillaea along its entire length until they reached an arched gateway leading to an extensive garden ablaze with every colour of the rainbow.

'Hullo!' a familiar voice greeted them from the top of the wall. 'We're on the look-out for you and you are ten minutes late.'

Andreas got down from behind the steering-wheel, smiling up at Martha who was perched on the top of the wall.

'Come down,' he ordered, 'and greet us properly. Your mother would never approve of a welcoming speech sitting astride a wall. Besides, you're spoiling the hibiscus.'

'There's masses and masses of it all over the place,' Martha told him before she disappeared from her precarious perch. 'Anyway, Susan is here with me, standing on the path to make sure I don't fall.'

The disembodied voice of her governess came from the other side of the wall. 'We've opened the gate for you, Andreas, so you can drive right in. Is Anna with you?'

'She is, indeed, and we are late because we stopped half-way to drink coffee with an old friend.'

There was no immediate reply and he got back into the car and drove through the arch into a wonderland of flowers.

The Villa Napa stood on a rocky ledge above its terraced garden with a plunging view over a forest of pines, cypress and cedar to the lush valley below. A mountain stream rushed down among the limestone, making a spectacular waterfall to one side of the house and on the other a large, open-air swimming-pool reflected the cloudless blue of the sky as in a mirror surrounded by flowers. Red and orange, blue and pink, they tumbled from troughs everywhere, while at the very end of the pool a yellow parasol and several reclining chairs were set out on the warm cream sandstone of the patio, waiting for Lara's guests.

Lara herself came towards them from the direction of the house looking incredibly lovely in a soft, flowing kaftan dappled with orange flowers, and as she held out her hand to them in greeting Anna imagined that all the sadness had vanished from her eyes. She looked a woman fulfilled as she kissed them on both cheeks in welcome, allowing her eyes to linger a fraction longer on Andreas as she led the way into the house.

'I'm so glad you could come,' she told Anna with the utmost sincerity. 'It would have been such a waste for Andreas to drive all this way alone when your mother is staying so near.' She hesitated only for a moment as they reached the open door. 'I haven't been able to get to see her yet, but we will try to go next week. Philip has not been well. I think the journey must have been too much for him, Andreas,' she added. 'We should have taken your advice and broken it at the Crescent Beach for a day or two, but he was so anxious to get home.'

There had been the merest hesitation before that final word, but already they were in the cool, spacious hall where the high, arched windows were shuttered against the heat of mid-day and a quiet reigned which could almost be felt

'He's waiting in the study,' Lara said.

'I'll take these in to him—they're magazines.' Andreas moved towards a white archway leading to another room. 'And he'd better see the papers before we sign them.'

'We've been talking business all morning,' Lara confessed, 'and I'm afraid I may have tired him. I thought the papers could wait a little, Andreas, till we have something to drink. Are you quite sure you can't stay for a meal with us? Well, perhaps not,' she added. 'Anna must be anxious to see her mother.'

Standing at the top of the two marble steps which went down into the lower hall, Anna was aware of a movement in the archway, and it had also alerted Andreas who turned with a stricken look to greet their host.

The tall, white-haired man who came slowly towards them was the man who had been sitting beside Lara in the front seat of the Mercedes when they had passed on the narrow track outside Prodhromos. The leonine head, the classic features, as if carved from ivory, suggested authority, but where he had looked upright and strong in the car he now came towards them leaning heavily on a stick, his broad shoulders hunched, his grey eyes darkened with pain.

Martha rushed towards him. 'Let me help you, Daddy.' she cried. 'Mummy says you must be careful of the steps.'

The concern in the young voice made him smile. 'The steps are not too much for me, Marty, but I will do better with your help.' He took his daughter's hand. 'And now you can introduce me to your new friend,' he suggested, meeting Anna's eyes as he crossed the floor.

'This is Miss Rossides,' Martha informed him primly. 'Her mother saved me when we fell in the swimming-pool before there was any water in it.'

Everybody laughed. Anna thought it was the first time she had ever heard Lara laugh spontaneously, and she looked up to see her silhouetted against a lovely old Tabriz carpet which hung against the stark white wall between the arches, thinking her more beautiful in that moment than she had ever been.

Philip Warrender and Anna shook hands.

'I've been waiting to meet you,' he said. 'Did you have a pleasant journey?'

'It renewed so many old memories,' she answered unguardedly. 'We spent much of the summer here in the past.'

'You couldn't have chosen a more beautiful spot,' he said, 'but now you must be ready for something cool to drink. What can I offer you?'

'She likes orange-juice,' Martha advised him. 'We drink it all the time at the hotel.'

Her father's eyebrows shot up in a quizzical expression that made her laugh. 'So, that's why you like being on the coast so much,' he said. 'You will turn into an orange, you know, one of these days.'

'Now you are teasing me,' Martha accused him delightedly. 'I couldn't really turn into an orange, could I?' She looked quickly at her mother.

'You're round enough.' Lara smiled. 'But I don't think that will happen, all the same. Can you bring a tray and ask Elpida for some plates?'

Anna noticed that she had made no effort to usurp her husband's role as host although he walked slowly and awkwardly to the cabinet in a corner which held the drinks.

'Whisky, Andreas?' he asked, looking at the younger man for the first time. 'Or is it too early in the day?'

Andreas seemed to rouse himself from an uneasy dream to answer him. 'I'm going to follow Anna's example and have orange-juice,' he decided, watching as Martha danced back into the room carrying a silver tray. 'Here, let me have that, nymph,' he added. 'You're going to spill something.'

'Only almonds,' she assured him, helping herself to a nut. 'Elpida's bringing the other things.'

A maid appeared with little dishes of sweetmeats which she placed on the side tables around the room. She was a shy, country girl with a round, beaming face and shining eyes, doing her best to please her new mistress, and Lara gave her a quick smile of encouragement as she hurried back to the kitchen through the second archway.

'This island is full of treasures, in more ways than one,' Lara declared. 'Do, please, sit down and we can talk for a while before you have to go.'

It all seemed so natural, the reflection of the usual happy home, yet Anna was aware of a certain amount of tension in the atmosphere, particularly when she looked at Andreas. He was helping their host with the drinks now, the set of his jaw harder than ever, his mouth stern as he moved about the room, and she wondered what he was thinking. What would any man think in the circumstances, she wondered, in love with a woman whose husband was his friend?

Somehow, she could not look at him for any length of time, seeing the pain in his eyes and the longing. Philip Warrender was ill—there could be no doubt about that— but he had been a strong man both physically and mentally and there would be every hope of his recovery. Surely there would be every hope!

They spoke of her mother and the nearness of the Masistas estate, 'It was no coincidence,' Lara explained. 'We wanted to be central yet not too far from the sea where Philip could swim, and we had been to the Troodos before.'

'On our honeymoon,' Philip put in, handing Anna a long crystal glass of freshly squeezed orange-juice.

'Nikos advised us about this villa,' Lara continued almost hastily. 'He has been very kind and decidedly helpful. We had many provisions, you see, because we did not want to be part of a holiday complex and we needed our privacy and a large garden, preferably with a pool.'

'You have everything here,' Anna agreed, glancing through the open patio doors to the blue-tiled swimming-pool which reflected an even bluer sky 'And you are so near the forest with its wonderful views.'

Tall poplars edged the garden in the north above a natural amphitheatre through which the infant river cut its way, making a dozen little waterfalls over the rock, and it was the murmur of flowing water which gave the Villa Napa its suggestion of peace, yet there could not be any real peace there if the people who lived in it were so hopelessly torn apart. Anna turned from her contemplation of the garden as Susan came into the room and sat down on the deep white settee beside her.

'What do you think of our new abode?' she asked perkily. 'Nice, isn't it? And not *too* far away from civilisation. It's a fabulous villa and everybody ought to be happy here.'

She was looking at Andreas, obviously wondering what part he would play in their lives now that Philip Warrender had returned.

Anna smoothed the cushion at her side with nervous fingers. 'Will you stay now that you have seen the mountains?' she asked.

'I don't know.' Susan glanced sharply in Lara's direction. 'It's a lot of work looking after a volatile child like Martha and trying to teach her text-book English into the bargain.'

'But surely with all the privileges you'll enjoy here, that can't be too hard,' Anna suggested.

'Perhaps not,' Susan allowed. 'And if I thought we would go to the beach most days it might be worthwhile, but it will all depend on what happens, of course.' She paused, following Philip's awkward movements across the room as he replenished their glasses. 'It's a terrible tragedy, isn't it? He was such a handsome man.'

When Anna did not reply she added boldly, 'It wasn't an accident, you know. He had some sort of incurable disease—some syndrome or other. I don't know much about it, but I don't think he'll ever recover and it's all rather sad.'

Anna sat upright among the cushions, all feeling gone out of her for a moment as she looked at the man she had just met and beyond him to where Andreas and Lara were deep in conversation, their heads bent as they studied the papers Andreas had brought with him from Limassol.

'If we sign these,' Lara suggested, looking up as her husband approached, 'Andreas can take them back with him. You may want to have a longer time to decide about the New York merger, though, so we'll keep that to one side.' She handed him a sheaf of papers. 'Whatever you say,' she suggested.

'I haven't made up my mind about the merger.' Philip turned to go back to his study. 'The other papers are of no great importance so I'll sign them right away.'

He was evidently still in full control of their business affairs, allowing him a dignity which he obviously appreciated, and Anna did not think that either of them would want to humiliate him in that way. The tragedy lay in the fact that they all respected each other and gratitude played a part, too, where Andreas was concerned.

When Philip returned with the signed documents Andreas sprang to his feet.

'Time to make a move,' he said with a hint of reluctance in his voice. 'This place is far too seductive,' he added. 'It has far too many attractions.'

Philip laughed as he handed back the papers. 'Thank you for bringing them,' he said, 'and don't be too long before you come back.'

Employer and employee exchanged confidential glances.

'Maybe next weekend,' Andreas suggested. 'I'll let you know.'

'Then we can have a picnic at the seaside!' Martha cried, slipping her hand into Anna's as they went towards the car 'Will you come, too?'

'I'll have to think about it 'Anna said gently. 'It may be difficult for me to get away.'

'Why the reluctance?' Andreas asked as he drove

through the gateway. 'You could easily delegate again, especially as you seem to have enjoyed today so far.'

The day wasn't over yet, but Anna felt as if a lifetime had passed since they had left Limassol that morning, driving into the mountains with no thought of sorrow in her heart.

'It's hard to believe,' she said. 'About Philip. He looks so strong and capable. I feel so sorry for them both.'

He swung the car round a sharp bend in the road, taking it far too quickly. 'Sorry doesn't cover what we feel, Anna,' he said harshly. 'It's a ghastly tragedy for everyone concerned.'

He had included himself in their heartache. He was part of it. Anna turned her head away, seeing the valley road through a mist of tears.

When they finally reached the farmhouse Dorothy greeted them on the loggia where she had been waiting for an hour. 'I thought you were never coming,' she told them. 'Have you had a good journey?'

'Splendid,' Andreas assured her, kissing her on both cheeks. 'We made a stop at Lara's new home to deliver some papers that had to be signed, killing two birds with one stone.' He held her at arms' length. 'You look glowing. What have you been doing with yourself since I saw you last?'

'Nothing more exciting than resting most of the day,' she told him.

'It has worked wonders,' he declared. 'What did I tell you about mountain air?'

'Mountain air and much kindness,' Dorothy reflected, kissing Anna on the cheek. 'What news have you brought?'

Her eagerness went deeper than trivial gossip on even the affairs of the Villa Severus.

'Nothing,' Anna said, disappointing her. 'We've been very busy, but apart from that most things have been the same.'

Dorothy searched her face for the truth. 'I thought,

perhaps—but never mind,' she added quickly. 'You're here and that's the main thing. Will you stay?'

'We've been invited to lunch.' Anna looked about her for any sign of Nikos or his father. 'Everyone seems to be busy,' she remarked.

'It's an early harvest this year.' Dorothy appeared to be concentrating on something else. 'I feel so well now,' she said. 'I could come home.'

Anna looked round sharply. 'You mustn't think of it.' she remonstrated. 'Remember what Doctor Ioannu said. The heat would be too much for you in June and July.'

Dorothy sighed. 'I suppose I must accept that,' she said, 'especially when everyone is being so kind and Helena and I do have a great many things in common.'

'I'm glad,' Anna said, feeling relieved. 'We have a message for you from John Malecos, by the way,' she added lightly. 'He threatens to pop in and see you one of these days'.

'He was here yesterday,' Dorothy's cheeks were faintly flushed with pink. 'He brought some flowers—and chocolates for Helena.'

Nikos and his father appeared at the far end of the loggia as Helena came from the house to welcome them. She had very little to say to Andreas, greeting him frigidly as she looked at her son. Kypros Masistas, however, was almost boisterous in his welcome.

'It's too long since we met, Andreas Phedonos,' he said, shaking him vigorously by the hand, 'but this is just like old times! You must come often now that you have found your way here. Do you still ski in the winter?'

Andreas shook his head. 'I haven't had much practice lately—much time for it, I suppose I mean, but when I was in Switzerland two years ago learning my trade I did manage some time in the mountains around Zurich. Perhaps I will get into shape again next winter.'

'You are here to stay, then?' Helena asked, evidently disappointed.

'For a while,' Andreas answered, amused. 'The

Crescent Beach is running quite smoothly, but we hope to build another hotel at Larnaca in the near future and perhaps one at Paphos if we can buy the necessary land.'

Nikos, who had been listening to his plans, sat down beside Anna. 'We have quite a tycoon on our hands,' he remarked. 'Where does he mean to start all this buying of land, do you think?'

'I don't know,' Anna said uncertainly, 'He'll be buying it for Lara, I expect. She's the tycoon—or, at least, her husband is.' She turned to face him. 'I've just met Philip and—nobody could help liking him,' she added.

'He's been ill, I understand.'

'Yes, very ill.'

Suddenly she was remembering the scene at the villa they had just left, the happiness that had overshadowed the pain, and the trust that Philip Warrender had in his wife.

Nikos rose to his feet as his mother led the way into the house. 'Time to eat!' he announced. 'We're earlier today because we have a buyer coming over from Nicosia to look at our crop, but he won't stay too long, I hope. After that we can have a swim or play some tennis, whichever you would like.'

'I haven't brought a swimsuit,' Anna said as they followed the others, 'and my tennis is very rusty.'

'For want of practice,' he decided, 'and we can easily find you something to swim in. The girls have discarded bikinis all over the place.'

'When do they come home?' she asked.

'June, I think—or is it July? They descend on us like a whirlwind and nothing is quite the same till they go back to school.'

It was said with affection because they were a closely knit family with a great deal in common and Nikos was particularly fond of the twins.

The meal they shared was a lavish one, set out in the family dining-room with the patio doors left open to let in the mountain air. The scent of jasmine and the hum of bees drifted in to them as they sat round the large oak table with Kypros presiding at the head and Helena at the far end near the folding doors which led through to the kitchens. Anna glanced across the table at her mother, thinking that she looked content in these pleasing surroundings with people she had known for much of her married life, and if she had another friend, or even an admirer, in John Malecos that was also good. It was a long time since she had appeared so happy.

Their coffee was served on the loggia as the sun slanted through the garden trees, and presently a car drew up to the front of the house, bringing Kypros reluctantly to his feet.

'If you can bear to tear yourself away, Nikos, my son, we'll get this inspection over and be done with it' he grumbled. 'It's bad for my digestion to be talking business so soon after a good meal when all I can think of is a satisfying smoke in an easy chair.' He looked down at Andreas. 'Care to come with us?' he asked.

'I'd like to very much.' Andreas got up to follow him. 'I won't get in the way of the bargaining,' he promised, 'but I'd like to look round, if I may.'

'You are welcome,' Kypros told him. 'Go anywhere you like. You know your way around.'

They went off together under the pergola where the heavy vine leaves dappled the pavement with light and shade and Helena excused herself to go into the house.

Anna moved to a chair nearer her mother, but for a moment she found nothing to say. The garden peace enveloped them with the all-pervading scent of jasmine dominating their senses until Dorothy looked round to say, 'You're very quiet. Has something gone wrong?'

Anna pulled her thoughts back from the Villa Napa with a considerable effort. 'No,' she lied for her mother's peace of mind, 'nothing has gone wrong. Things are working out quite smoothly at home.'

'I wasn't thinking about the hotel, I was thinking about you,' Dorothy said. 'You look—sad.'

'You know I'm not sad.' Anna's eyes followed the line of the pergola to where it met the terrace wall. 'It's lovely to see you looking so well and—contented.'

'That wasn't what I meant,' Dorothy persisted. 'I was thinking about you and Andreas—about you making your peace with one another.'

Anna looked down at her clasped hands. 'Maybe we've done that,' she said, 'or perhaps we just don't want to argue any more.' Her voice was not quite steady. 'We've come a long way, Mama, in understanding, at least.'

'And what have you discovered?'

'That—perhaps we can be friends.'

'Is that enough?'

'It is—as much as I can expect. Oh, Mama, I don't want to talk about it yet. I can't bear to talk about it.'

Dorothy put out her hand. 'Take your time,' she said gently, 'but come to me if it gets too hard.'

'I promise I will.' Anna brushed the hair back from her forehead. 'And now, what about a walk? Down across the garden will do.'

'I can manage farther than that,' Dorothy declared proudly. 'We'll go as far as the cottage and back.'

'Do you still want to go there to stay eventually?'

'Not just yet, but perhaps before the twins come home. Helena will want her family to herself.'

'I thought you were getting on very well.'

'We are, but I don't want to intrude for too long. I'd be happy at the cottage with someone to look after me for a while. Then, in the winter, I can come home.'

They walked across the estate, down through the orange groves where late blossom and ripened fruit hung together on the trees, and past the vines to the carobs and olives on the slope of the hill. It was a lush picture, tended carefully by father and son with their hopes firmly rooted in the future. They saw Nikos and Kypros talking to the prospective buyer of the lemon crop, but Andreas appeared to have gone his own way, probably doubling back to the house through the vineyard or even climbing the hill for a better view of the valley below.

Andreas was first back at the house, settling himself on the loggia to await their return, his thoughts busy in the past as he looked down to the river with the tall poplars growing along its banks.

'Ah. You have returned,' Helena said as she came from the house to join him. 'Have you left my husband and son bargaining? They are so wrapped up in the work of the estate,' she went on without waiting for his answer, 'and Nikos has made us very proud. He is a good son and all this will one day be his.' Her gaze swept across the lush land on either side of them 'It is a prosperous estate, as you can see, and an excellent inheritance. All he needs now is a suitable wife.'

She paused, and after a moment Andreas enquired, 'Have you someone in mind?'

'Anna would be my choice,' Helena said determinedly. 'She is the sort of girl he needs, sensible and of a good background, and we are definately encouraged by what we see. They are *very* fond of each other. In fact, I would say they are in love.'

He thrust his hands deep into his trousers pockets, not trusting himself to speak immediately.

'Of course,' Helena said, 'we must leave them to make their own decision, but I think the result is inevitable. Anna knows how comfortable her mother would be here—we have already offered her a cottage on the estate—and she certainly has her mother's interests at heart. Not that I would force the issue, of course, but it would solve a great many problems all round.'

'Anna may wish to keep the hotel,' he pointed out.

'That wouldn't be necessary or desirable,' Helena informed him. 'She would have a full and contented life here.'

'Certainly a full one,' he agreed. 'Do they intend to become engaged?' Helena considered the question for a moment before she answered him deliberately, 'In the very near future, I would say. Neither of them must want to wait and Anna knows that we will welcome her into our family with open arms and a great deal of pride.'

'If pride comes into it,' he said coldly, 'I think you are right about Anna. She will make a good daughter-in-law. And now, if you will excuse me, Kiria Masistas, I'd like to take a look at my car. It was behaving badly on the way over from Prodhromos and I don't want to break down on our way home.'

'Ask one of the men to help you,' Helena advised. 'They know quite a lot about cars.'

All the way back to Limassol Andreas was unusually quiet, sitting behind the steering-wheel with a grim look on his face and totally uncommunicative as they passed through the little villages on the hill roads and came to the plane where the orange groves lay peacefully behind their screens of poplars, their golden fruit bright in the setting sun. In field after field the rich red soil had given of its bounty and already another crop was being planted in its place.

'Do you wish me to come in and see that everything has gone according to plan?' Andreas asked as they neared their destination

'I don't think there's any need.' She felt hurt and neglected. 'Thank you for taking me to the Masistas'. It's been a very long day.'

When she reached her own room there were tears in her eyes, tears of hurt and disappointment, but what was the use of crying for the past? She had the future to look to and the decisions she had to make would be considered with that in mind.

Determinedly she closed her bedroom door, telling herself that nothing else mattered but her mother's happiness and her own ability to cope.

CHAPTER SEVEN

SHE saw her mother again the following weekend, but it was Nikos who came to drive her back to Stroumbi. He was in high spirits, having worked hard to bring in a considerable harvest, shipping much of it direct to their agents in Great Britain, and his father was proud of him.

'I have a surprise for you,' he said helping her into his car.

'Tell me,' she encouraged him.

'Not likely! It's a deadly secret at present but you won't have to wait too long after we get home.'

Home to the estate, he meant, already including her in his personal background.

'Nikos,' she said carefully, 'if it has anything to do with family—an intimate celebration or anything like that— I'm sure it would be best if you counted me out. I could spend the day quietly with my mother if you have arranged something away from the estate.'

'We will be going away and your mother is coming with us so don't go on arguing. The trouble with you is that you can't wait for a surprise!' he added lightly.

'But it is intriguing, Nikos, to say the least,' she laughed, 'and I'm naturally curious.'

'It's a sort of a celebration.' He wasn't very good at keeping secrets. 'You'll be happy to go.'

'Oh? Well, in that case, I accept. Where are we going?'

'One of your favourite spots.' He glanced at her sideways. 'Somewhere you've been often enough before.'

'I can hardly wait!'

She was determined not to ask any more questions, suspecting that Helena had made the arrangements, whatever they were.

'Are the twins at home?'

164

'Not yet. They don't break up till the end of June.'

'No—I remember you saying.'

So it couldn't be a birthday celebration, at least not for his sisters.

It rained a little as they approached the mountains, fine, refreshing rain shimmering on the orchard leaves as the sun hid behind a gigantic cloud ahead of them.

'Have you thought about what I said?' Nikos asked as he negotiated a sudden bend in the road.

'About going to wherever you are going?'

'No, not that. About marrying me in the near future.'

They were winding up a steep hill with a monastery on the horizon and a deep river valley falling away to the plain below.

'I've thought about it, Nikos,' she answered slowly, her eyes on the level stretch of cultivated land beneath them, 'and I know it can't be in the near future, if at all. I'm sorry,' she hastened to apologise, 'but I have so many other decisions to make, so much to resolve before——'

'Before you can think of your own happiness?' he broke in.

'I didn't mean that. What I was trying to say is that—I'm not ready for love yet.'

Another love, she meant, if that could ever be.

'I know there's someone else and I think it's Andreas.' He was fully convinced now. 'But that's all gone by the board, hasn't it? He's definitely not for you and it would be better if you forgot all about him.'

'I know.' She turned her head away, looking towards the mountains. 'But you told me you didn't want second best, Nikos, and that would be the way it would be. I can't let you go on hoping like this, planning for a future that could be perfect for you with the right wife.'

'You could be that wife.' He swung the car into the long stretch of main road before Stroumbi. 'There's nobody else I want, though I suppose I can't go on waiting for ever. There's also your mother to consider,' he added pointedly. 'She could be happy in our family circle for the rest of her life.'

'That was unfair, Nikos!' she cried. 'I think about her comfort and happiness all the time, as you know very well, but if she thought I was making—sacrifices, it wouldn't help at all. I'm being terribly blunt,' she added gently, 'but it wouldn't be fair to lie to you about how I feel.'

He frowned at the road ahead. 'We're in a dreadful muddle,' he admitted. 'I still want you and you haven't had time to think straight, so I can still go on hoping, I guess. It's something I'm quite good at, by the way, so don't try to persuade me otherwise.'

'I wish I could,' Anna sighed. 'It's so unfair, Nikos!'

'Let me be the judge of that.' He turned his head to smile at her. 'Today we are going to enjoy ourselves in spite of all you have just said.'

'I'm not usually such a wet blanket!'

'I know you're not, and today will be just splendid.'

He drove on throught the mountain villages with masses of wild flowers besieging the narrow, rutted roads and bougainvillaea blazing over ancient walls. Donkeys and wandering goats strayed across their path, while mountain sheep turned to stare at them before they sprang off into the scrub land and disappeared. At Pano Panayia, where the dirt roads fanned down into the valleys, the sun came out again in full strength and Nikos looked up at it with a smile.

'A good omen,' he predicted. 'Everything is going to turn out well, after all!'

A car turned into the valley ahead of them. It was the white Mercedes, apparently heading for the estate.

'Nikos, what's going on?' Anna turned in her seat to look at her companion. 'Is this what's been arranged— the Warrenders and Susan and Martha?'

'Particularly Martha,' he grinned. 'It's her birthday.'

'I didn't know. Nobody mentioned it ——'

'I told you it was a surprise. They phoned at the beginning of the week asking us to join them, and your mother seemed particularly delighted. She likes Lara, I think, and nobody could resist Martha for very long. She's been on the phone every day since to make sure we haven't forgotten our promise.'

'Will—everybody be there?' Anna meant Andreas, surprised that she had not heard from him about the arrangements. 'Everyone that can come, I mean.'

'I guess so. It's going to be quite a party!'

'You can tell me now where we are going,' she suggested.

'Oh, well—we're going on a rather special picnic to Khrysokhou Bay.'

'So that's why you told me not to forget my swimsuit?' Anna laughed. 'I could hardly appear at the baths in the nude.'

'Aphrodite did!' he laughed in return. 'This seems to have been a long-promised event as far as Martha is concerned and she's been looking forward to it. So has Susan.'

'You like Susan a lot,' she suggested.

'Oh, she's all right, A bit giggly, but all right. She plays a good game of tennis, if that's anything to go by, and she hasn't any ties. She has no family in England, I understand.' He swung the car through the estate entrance, looking ahead with enthusiasm. 'Even my father is coming with us,' he said, 'and that *must* be an event!'

He drove swiftly after the Mercedes, catching up with it as it slowed at the front of the house where Helena was waiting in a cream woollen suit with a fixed smile on her face, ready to be introduced to Lara and her family.

Martha was first out of the car, skipping round the bonnet to greet Anna and her companion with complimentary enthusiasm.

'You're just in time,' she cried. 'We're all ready to go to the beach!' Lara got out of the Mercedes to shake hands with Helena and Kypros, who had appeared in the doorway behind his wife, while Anna was aware of

Philip Warrender looking on from the back seat of the roomy automobile with Susan by his side.

'I'll go and have a word with my mother,' she suggested. 'I hope this won't be too much for her.'

'I don't think it will,' Nikos said, 'but go and see for yourself.'

Dorothy Rossides was coming down the staircase from her own room when her daughter looked up at her to verify Nikos' statement and there could be no denying the fact that her short stay in the mountains had produced an almost miraculous result. The pallor had receded from her skin and her English wild-rose complexion coloured her cheeks again, like a faint blush. Her hair, not yet turned grey, was the colour of sun-bleached corn and the blue-grey dress she wore in defiance of her widowhood complemented her smiling sapphire eyes.

'Mama, you look radiant!' Anna exclaimed. 'Never have I seen such an improvement in anyone in so short a time!'

'Flatterer!' Dorothy returned, coming down the few remaining stairs to kiss her. 'You'll be telling me next that I don't look a day over forty!'

'I wouldn't go that far!' Anna laughed. 'Don't tell me the mountain air alone has made such an enormous change!'

'The mountains, and so much else besides,' Dorothy confessed.

'Such as?'

'Oh, things like care and friendship and—and good company.' The deepening colour in her cheeks was now a definite blush. 'John has been coming up almost every evening. John Malecos,' she added as if Anna might not understand.

'So—you old dark horse!' Anna met the glowing sapphire eyes with deep understanding in her own, 'How long has *this* been going on?'

' "This" is only a very good friendship,' her mother

informed her, 'so you mustn't read anything more into it than that.'

'I won't.' Anna's mind was in sudden turmoil. 'Is John Malecos coming on Martha's picnic?'

'I'm not quite sure. He was certainly invited. I think everybody was!'

Except Andreas, Anna thought, but it was strange that Martha had not insisted on him being there.

'We are ready to start,' Helena said, coming back into the hall. 'Take a jacket with you, Dorothy. We can't risk you getting cold.'

The Warrenders had obviously provided the picnic lunch, but Helena had organised her own contribution to the feast, hastening to the kitchens to produce a basket covered by a white cloth which she gave to Nikos to put in her car.

'You'll come with us,' she told Dorothy, 'and Nikos can bring Anna. It's an open car and not at all suitable for you when you have just been ill,' she added.

Anna and her mother exchanged glances, but Helena's arrangements had evidently been made as soon as the invitation from Lara had been accepted.

'See you at Lachi!' Anna smiled. 'We can talk for hours once we get there.'

They followed the valley road to Magoúnda and on to Pólis to find the ancient city-state of Marion lazily asleep in the morning sun. Standing on its commanding height a short distance from the sea and up to its knees in orchards, Pólis was a popular tourist rendezvous, but the rain of early morning had dampened the enthusiasm of all but the most intrepid visitors and once they were out again on the coast road they were almost on their own. The three cars made a small procession along the peninsula, the Mercedes in front with Lara driving, the estate car bringing up the rear, and Nikos' roadster in between.

'We should have the bay practically to ourselves,' Nikos said. 'Most people will be at the tombs on a day like this after a morning's rain.'

He left the asphalted road, taking an unsurfaced track to a magnificent viewpoint above the bay where sun and sea sparkled through a verdant landscape of carob and eucalyptus trees and the pungent scent of myrtle filled the air.

Anna knew it well because she had come there often enough as a child to climb down the ravine with its legendary cave where limpid water fell amid wild figs and trailing plants into a natural basin hollowed from the rock. The traditional Spring of Aphrodite, whose water made those who drank it lovesick!

She knew that the true Fontana Amorosa lay farther along the coast, but this beautiful ravine had always remained a rendezvous for lovers and she had once come here with Andreas long ago.

So long ago that he had probably forgotten all about it. She gazed into the crystalline spring, a sigh escaping her lips as Nikos helped her down the path towards the beach.

The other cars had disgorged their passengers along the shore after Lachi and Martha ran quickly to greet them.

'Where have you been?' she demanded.

'Looking for Love!' Nikos grinned, hoisting her on to his shoulders. 'We'll take you to the Baths some other time.'

Kypros and Lara were helping Philip along the beach.

'We're going to swim,' Martha announced. 'My Daddy used to be a champion swimmer,' she added proudly, 'and he can still beat Andreas!'

Andreas was conspicuous by his absence although he might have been expected to attend a small girl's birthday picnic, especially a small girl who apparently adored him.

Slipping off the cotton sun-dress she wore over her swimsuit, Anna waded into the sea, swimming strongly when Nikos joined her.

'I'll race you to the island,' he challenged, but she shook her head. 'Too dangerous. I know this shore,' she said, but perhaps she was just waiting for Andreas to appear.

Philip and Lara swam together far out into the bay, Lara's scarlet costume contrasting vividly with the sun-dazzled aquamarine water, Philip's silver head visible for a long time above the surf. He was evidently in his element in the sea, untramelled by any hint of paralysis as he lay on his back with his face to the sun enjoying a freedom he was denied on land. Anna swam away, leaving them together as she headed back towards the shore where Nikos was teaching Martha to dog-paddle while Susan looked on. She could see Dorothy farther along the beach, sitting in the shade of a carob tree talking to a man in white shorts with a brilliantly striped towel across his shoulders.

Andreas? No, the newcomer was not tall enough. Slowly she went towards them, recognising John Malecos who was an old friend of the family, widowed many years.

Ti kanete? he greeted her. 'I'm glad you were able to spare a day off to visit your mother,' he added, looking down at Dorothy with deep affection. 'She misses you.'

'We've got to come to terms with the summer heat,' Anna reminded him, 'and it's so beautiful up here in the mountains. I see you've been invited to the birthday lunch.'

'Marty went round inviting everyone in sight,' he smiled. 'Now that she knows how to use the telephone there's no holding her back!'

Anna sat down beside him. 'It's ages since we met,' she remembered. 'Are you still working in Nicosia?'

He shook his head. 'I've retired. Time I was settling down to some relaxation, I thought, and the business seems to be running itself these days. I still keep the bachelor flat in Nicosia, but I've bought a place at Nikos near the monastery. We all migrate to the hills eventually,' he decided. 'I'm trying to persuade your mother to come and see my modest abode while she is with the Masistas' and she has all but promised to do so. If you were not such a busy young woman,' he added, 'I'd ask you to bring her along.'

Anna glanced at her mother. Dorothy's sapphire eyes were glowing, her cheeks prettily flushed.

'Perhaps Andreas would bring me,' she said. 'Or Nikos.'

'Any time!' John prepared to go for his swim. 'I think Philip and Lara are going too far out,' he said. 'I must warn them.'

Five minutes later a familiar car drew into the parking lot behind them and Andreas got out, striding across the beach to where they sat.

'It wasn't too easy to find you,' he said, sitting down beside them. 'I was looking for Nikos' car.'

'We left it up at the headland, on the dust road,' Anna explained, 'and walked down through the ravine.'

'To the falls,' he said, meeting her gaze directly. 'Did they prove anything?'

'Aphrodite must have been somewhere else!' Anna said lightly. 'Besides, I've been there before.'

'With me,' he said.

And now she had gone there with Nikos, to the legendary spring which had always been a meeting-place for lovers although the memory of her first visit there with Andreas was still strong in her heart. He had thought of that visit, too, but the poignant simplicity of first love could be no more than a memory to him now.

'Are you going to swim?'she asked.

'What else?' He stood up to consider the water. 'Will you come?'

She smoothed her swimsuit, which had already dried in the sun. 'I've been in already.'

'Does that matter? We used to swim all day,' he reminded her.

'Go with him,' Dorothy said. 'I'll be fine just sitting

here in the shade.'

Anna hesitated.

'Are you ready?' Andreas asked, holding out his hand.

She could not very well refuse him. She did not want to refuse, but she ignored his proffered hand, getting to her feet unaided to run with him towards the sea, her heart suddenly light and glad.

They swam together for half-an-hour, the sun warm on their backs, the sea a vast open blue plain isolating them from the land. The tiny waves they made sparkled around them, and when they floated idly to rest for a while Andreas said, 'If your mother eventually goes to stay at Stroumbi will you go with her?'

'You're asking me if I'm going to marry Nikos.'

'That was the general idea, wasn't it?'

'No. I will have to make my own decision.' She caught her breath. 'I haven't done that yet.'

Lying there in the cool blue water by his side such a decision seemed impossible because nothing—nothing at all could ever take the place of what had been for her the first bitter-sweet experience of love.

'Will you tell me when you make up your mind? I know it would be best for Mama.'

She turned on her side to look at him. 'You don't know at all,' she accused him. 'You *think* it would be best for her, but she has a will of her own, remember. She—could marry again.'

'Aha!' he exclaimed, paddling idly. 'You surprise me. Is romance really in the offing?'

She hesitated.

'You can tell me,' he encouraged her. 'I'm one of the family, in case you have forgotten.'

'You're being facetious;'

'Not really.' The smile left his face. 'You know I have her interests very much at heart and I believe she now trusts me. Has someone proposed to her?'

'Not yet, but I think John Malecos will eventually.'

He whistled. 'You don't really surprise me,' he

decided. 'She is still a very attractive woman. Are you jealous?'

'Jealous? Of course not! I want her happiness more than anything else.'

'What would you do with the villa? Sell it?'

The question made her angry. 'No, I would never part with it, even if I had to live there alone.' He left that unanswered, striking out towards the shore.

'Time to go,' he said. 'Lara and Philip are already on the beach.'

The picnic lunch they shared had been specially prepared by Lara to include food which would please both her Greek and English guests. Many of the dishes were regional specialities of Greece and Turkey and even the drinks she served beforehand were presented with a selection of appetisers. *Mezedabia* was a favourite with the men, and *beccaficos* and *dolmades* went down well with everyone once Martha had explained carefully that she had helped to stuff the little vine leaves herself. The desserts, however, were the final *coup de grâce*. Slices of nuts and almonds in currant jelly, *kadaif*, an oriental honey-cake, and *halvas*, to be followed inevitably by *rahat-loukoum*, the local Turkish Delight, were sampled eagerly as they laughed and lounged in the sun.

'I feel as stuffed as the vine leaves!' Nikos declared, biting into a second square of Turkish Delight. 'We ought not to eat in the middle of the day.'

Susan, who was sitting beside him, laughed. 'You look as if you could eat any time,' she said, 'but perhaps playing so much tennis helps to slim you down.'

'You play quite a lot, I understand.' He regarded her with interest. 'Do you miss the Crescent Beach?'

'Quite often, but it isn't really far to go down for a game now and then.' She looked at him suggestively. 'Perhaps you could offer me a lift next time you go?' she said. 'I wouldn't expect you to partner me, of course. It would be just for the chance to play.'

'What about Martha?' he asked.

'I do have time off—once a week, actually,'

'If I can make it,' Nikos said, 'I will.'

Anna, who had been listening idly, wondered what Lara would do without Susan's help even for a day now that she had Philip to look after, but perhaps that was a question Lara never asked herself. Perhaps she had already acknowledged the fact that Susan wouldn't stay in the mountains for a moment longer than it suited her and that one day she would have to cope with Martha by herself. It would not be for long, however, because Martha was due to go to boarding school in the autumn and no doubt Susan was well aware of the fact.

They played games on the beach, had another swim in the wide, blue bay and finally decided that it was time to go home.

'I must go straight back,' Anna said regretfully. 'It has been a wonderful day.'

Andreas had been lounging on the sand beside her mother. 'Let me take you,' he suggested. 'I have to be back at the Crescent Beach by six o'clock.'

Anna looked along the beach. 'I came with Nikos——'

'What difference? It will save him the double journey.'

'It does seem a sensible idea,' Dorothy said. 'Helena has invited everybody back to the house, but I suppose you have to go.'

'Must do!' Anna said 'Elli has the evening off and Paris hates to make decisions on his own.'

Nikos came up with Susan who still wore her swimsuit.

'We're going in for a final dip,' she said. 'How about you, Anna?'

'I'd love to, but I have to be on my way.' Anna looked at Nikos. 'Andreas has offered to take me back,' she explained. 'It will save you the double journey.'

He looked disgruntled. 'Why can't you wait?' he demanded. 'I could get you back in no time—just over an hour, anyway.'

'I would save you a lot of trouble if I went with

Andreas,' she pointed out.

'You must please yourself.' He turned to go down the beach. 'I'll see you some time next week.'

'Was that a lovers' tiff?' Andreas asked when they were finally in his car driving towards Pólis.

'It was a sensible alternative to him driving to Limassol and back when there was no need to.'

'I thought I detected a hint of discord.' He settled down behind the steering-wheel, his smile faintly amused. 'But let's forget about Nikos for a moment and talk about Mama. You said once that her future was all-important to you and now you know that it is important to me, too. I have no other ties, Anna, and I want to look after her, if I can.'

'There will be no need for that if she marries John Malecos,' she pointed out. 'He is quite able to look after her, but thank you, all the same, for offering.'

He gave her a fleeting glance before returning his attention to the road. 'It will leave you very much alone.'

She had thought of that but hadn't come to terms with it, so far. 'I'm young enough to cope,' she said, 'and I've already told you that I don't mean to give up the hotel. I know you hoped to buy it when you first came back—you and Lara—but that isn't on. I don't mean to sell.'

They were through Pólis, driving along the main highway where the traffic was thick.

'When I first returned I thought to make it my home again,' he said slowly, 'but we can forget that now. I have the flat at Paphos which suits my bachelor habits very well, and I occupy a suite at the Crescent Beach which is quite enough for me for the time being.'

The hilly, picturesque road claimed his attention for a moment, giving her time to digest what he had just said, and it seemed that he was telling her quite plainly that he had no intention of marrying until the woman he loved was free. Somehow, she would have expected nothing less of him.

'I'm sure everything will turn out—right for you in the

end,' she answered automatically, but how could it when Lara was so desperately and tragically involved?

'I hope so, too' he agreed, 'but it seems that I have a long way to go. Keep the hotel for the time being, Anna, but remember my offer and perhaps we might be able to co-operate a little more. There's going to be vast changes at Candy's Place, for instance, and if we don't work together that might be unfortunate. On the other hand, the excavations could very well prove an asset if we shared our responsibilities.'

'It looks as if we haven't much choice in that respect,' she told him, thinking how much happier the situation would have been if he hadn't loved someone else. 'Our decision will rest with the authorities, I suppose, though it might be fun sharing in the dig.'

'It would be tremendous fun and lots of interest for our guests. Yours are more the type who would want to help and not spend all their time frying themselves in the sun.'

'There would be interest from the Crescent Beach, too,' she said. 'It would be something quite different for most of them.'

He looked down at her for an instant, at her hair flying behind her in the breeze and the sparkle of enthusiasm in her eyes.

'The old Anna,' he said beneath his breath.

When they passed Stroumbi she thought of the others following behind them, glad that her mother seemed to be happy enough on the estate for the time being, glad, too, that she had the friendship of John Malecos to shield her from too much domination by Helena, who was accustomed to rule.

Andreas had abandoned the mountains and had come straight back by the main highway, skirting Paphos to reach the coast road and a clear run into Limassol.

Driving along Makarios Avenue to avoid the busier town centre he suggested abruptly, 'I want you to come to me if anything goes wrong, Anna. It's what you would have done if things had been different.'

'Spoken with true brotherly concern!' she acknowledged, trying to sound indifferent.

'If you like,' he agreed, turning on to the coast road.

'It could work both ways,' she suggested. 'If you ever needed my help——'

'I would ask for it,' he assured her.

She looked out across the bay.

'The sea is quite rough,' she observed to ease an awkward pause. 'The wind must have got up after we left Pólis.'

'It looks nasty,' he agreed. 'We may be in for a stormy night.'

When they reached the Villa Severus most of the guests had left the beach and the sun-umbrellas were flapping in the wind.

'Paris should have put them down as soon as the wind got up,' Anna said, frowning. 'He's not generally so careless, but perhaps he told Hannibal to do it and between them they forgot.'

Andreas turned the car in at the gates.

'Don't come down,' she said. 'I can manage quite well from here.'

He drove on without taking her advice, slowing as they reached the front of the villa where the pick-up was parked, together with several hired cars.

'Will you come in?' she asked. 'I'll fix you a drink,'

He got out from behind the steering-wheel to reach for her case which he had put in the back of the car.

'Only for a minute,' he said. 'We'll talk some more in the morning when we've had another look at the excavations.'

Ahead of them the doors stood open and Paris came towards them across the hall.

'We wondered when you would come,' he said, looking at Andreas. 'There's been a telephone call.'

'For me?' Andreas looked surprised.

'From the Crescent Beach,' Paris said. 'Would you get in touch with them immediately?'

Andreas shrugged his shoulders.

'I would have liked that drink,' he said.

'It may be nothing important,' Anna suggested, 'and you could phone through from here.'

He nodded.

'In my office,' she said. 'I'll take a quick look round out here to see that everything is in order.'

He went towards the office, closing the door behind him, and she walked quickly across the loggia where most of her guests were still sitting at the tea tables contemplating an unfriendly sea. A word here and there was expected of her, but she was back in the hall when Andreas reappeared in the office doorway.

'Andreas!' She was at his side in a moment. 'What's wrong?'

'There's been an accident.' He was looking beyond her, his composure utterly shattered, his expression frozen in shock. 'Philip,' he said. 'He's been drowned. Remember Susan saying they were going for a last swim——'

Anna stood gazing at him for what seemed an eternity. 'I know what this must mean to you,' she acknowledged, at last, recognising his friendship with both Lara and her husband. 'You will go back, of course, to be with Lara.'

'Right away,' he said between his teeth. 'This is terrible.'

'Do you want me to come with you?'

He hesitated. 'There wouldn't be any point, unless you are worried about Mama. She wasn't there, by the way. She had gone back to the estate with John Malecos and Marty before it happened.'

'How could it have happened?' Her voice seemed to fade away. 'He was such a strong swimmer ——'

'Cramp,' Andreas said grimly. 'It can attack anybody and perhaps the sea had turned rough as it did here. I don't know the details.'

'Can I make you something to eat before you go?'

He shook his head. 'There isn't time, but you could do

something for me over at the Crescent Beach.'

'Anything—you know that.'

'I have an agent coming at six o'clock. Could you see him and explain? He's from Lemmington Travel and I can't get in touch with him because I don't know where he's staying. Tell him as much as you need to and ask him to leave an address. I'll be in touch.'

'Would you like me to give him a meal over here?'

'No need. He can eat at the Crescent. I forgot all about him when I phoned through there just now, but I suppose he's important. My God, Anna, I feel as if I'm going out of my mind and I don't know what this will do to Lara. She was on the beach when it happened. She didn't go in a second time.'

'Do you know if Nikos and his mother were there?'

'Apparently Nikos got him out so we have that to thank him for, at least.'

'It must have been some sort of seizure.'

'I think so.' He kissed her on the cheek as they reached the door. 'Thanks for coping,' he said.

When he had gone she tried to pull her thoughts together, but it was no use. Nothing seemed real except this appalling tragedy and the stark agony on Andreas' face. He must be wishing now that he had never left Khrysokhou Bay, although he could have done no more than Nikos had done to help, but he could have been with Lara.

For the next few hours she seemed to move in a dream, doing everything automatically, meeting the spruce young agent from Lemmington Travel as Andreas had requested and explaining to him as best she could, and coming back to the Villa Severus to wait for the expected telephone call from Pólis, which seemed as if it never would come.

It was ten o'clock before the office phone rang, sounding in her ears like the knell of doom.

'Yes, Andreas?' she asked, but it was John Malecos at the far end of the line.

'Andreas asked me to call you,' he said, 'and I wanted to reassure you about your mother. She's very shocked, of course, but we have managed to get her to rest for a while.' He paused. 'Otherwise, there is nothing more to be done,' he added. 'We are all very upset, as you can imagine, and Andreas has taken Lara and Martha back to Pedhoulas to the villa. Tomorrow there will be an inquest, I expect.'

It was like something out of a bad dream with all the details hopelessly obscure.

'You're back at the estate,' she guessed. 'Will you stay there overnight?'

'I've been invited,' he said. 'Yes, I think I'll stay.'

'Thank you, John,' she said, putting the receiver back on its rest.

It was two days before she saw Andreas again. He came to the door of the office while she was busy typing menu cards, standing there without attracting her attention until she had typed the final card, and when she looked up she could see what the last two days had done to him. He looked haggard and sad, and most of his habitual assurance had disappeared.

'You haven't slept,' she guessed, rising to meet him. 'Sit down for a moment and I'll get you something to drink.'

'Tea will do,' he said, thrusting a hand through his thick black hair as he sank on to the settee beside the window. 'I had to come.'

The confession seemed utterly natural in the circumstances because he had told her only two days ago that they must depend upon one another in a crisis. She ordered the tea.

'I've come to ask you a favour,' he said. 'Will you go to Lara? I've brought her down to the Crescent because Pedhoulas was too full of memories for her.'

'Do you want me to go across now?' She put the menu cards to one side.

'If you will. I have to go to Limassol right away. It's a

nasty business getting everything straightened out, but at least I can save her that bit of it.' Paris came in with a tea tray set for two. 'I don't think she has realized it yet, although she is quite level-headed in other respects, and we're playing it down a little because of Martha who was just getting to know Philip again. It's a damnable shame—such an utter waste! He knew he hadn't long to live, but I don't think he wanted to go that way. It's a devil of a shock—the utter suddenness of it—and it will be a while before Lara can come to terms with it.' He left the cup of tea she had poured for him on the side table untouched. 'It's knocked me for six and I don't know what to say to her. I can't even offer her advice.'

'Not now,' Anna agreed, 'but she will need you in the end.'

'I think she needs another woman to talk to at the present moment.' He looked through the open window to the sea. 'Susan's no good. I think she would only irritate Lara with her trite observations about life and death. You would listen.'

'I'll do what I can, you know that.' She put a hand on his shoulder, longing to take him into the comfort of her arms. 'Finish your tea and I'll see you when you get back from Limassol.'

He stood up, watching as she crossed the hall to make her way along the beach.

When she left the shelter of the loggia the wind buffeted her, a tiresome wind sweeping in across the bay, warm but irritating, blowing the loose sand in her face. Beyond the breakwater the waves followed each other in endless procession to dash themselves against the stone barrier which protected the small pleasure craft, while along the line of the horizon the sky was already dark.

The Crescent Beach was full of people, laughing and relaxing on the sheltered terraces where the wind could not reach them, people on holiday waiting for the next meal or the next drink or even the next romance. Anna knew that she would not find Lara there and hurried inside.

A white-uniformed porter met her in the vast entrance hall. 'Can I help you, madam?'

'Would you ask Mrs Warrender if she would see me? I'm from the Villa Severus, next door,' she explained.

'I thought I recognised you.' His white teeth flashed in a charming smile. 'Mrs Warrender has gone to her room. I'll phone her.'

While she waited Anna thought how different the two hotels were, each with its own idea of service. The Crescent Beach was everything a four-star hotel should be with its highly trained staff in their immaculate uniforms, but it was strangely impersonal, while the Villa Severus still remained a home.

'Mrs Warrender will see you, madam. Will you go straight up? Her suite is on the first floor—number 407.'

In the lift Anna wondered what she could possibly say to Lara in this crisis in her life. Words were inadequate, pity impossible, although she felt both pity and sympathy for this older woman who had suddenly been brought face to face with tragedy in this traumatic way. Lara could never have expected such a swift ending to her married life even if the thought of her eventual freedom had crossed her mind when she had found herself in love with someone else.

The lift came to a silent halt on the first floor, the doors sliding open to reveal Lara's suite straight ahead. It was a life of absolute luxury, she supposed, to which Lara had become accustomed over the years, but now she might even be regretting it when it had kept her from establishing a true home until recently.

She knocked on the door.

'It's open. Come in!' Lara sounded tired. 'I've rung down for some tea. You'll wait for a while?'

She had been half-way to the door and now she turned to lead the way back into her sitting-room with the light full on her face. Anna held her breath. Like Andreas, she looked as if she had not slept for days. She was still immaculate, but the signs of strain were everywhere, in the tell-tale lines about her mouth and in the deeper sadness of her eyes.

'Andreas asked me to come,' Anna said. 'It seemed better than phoning once I knew you were here.'

Martha came through from an inner room, a much subdued Martha who had only a wan smile to offer her mother's visitor.

'Susan wants to play tennis,' she said half-heartedly, picking up a racquet from a chair.

'I think you should,' Lara said. 'There's time before dinner and you've been sitting in a car for most of the morning. Find Susan and tell her we'll be staying here for a day or two.'

When her daughter had closed the door behind her she turned to Anna. 'I find it difficult to think,' she confessed, 'especially about the things that concern us most, and sometimes I wonder when I'll wake up out of this dreadful bad dream. It has all happened so swiftly, Anna—so cruelly. Philip thought he had a year, at least, to live as a family again, That's the bitter bit, not being able to offer him sanctuary in the end. We were both so happy about the idea of Pedhoulas and our villa in the mountains where he had always wanted to be, and as it turned out he had little more than a week. I brought him from Rome when the doctors said they could do no more for him, but I know he wanted that year more than anything else. He wanted to see Martha grow up—he wanted her to appreciate the things he liked even though he had always worked too hard to enjoy them himself. It was the kind of man he was.'

The rush of words told their own story, Anna realised. The floodgates of grief had been opened and all Lara's pent up anguish had come rushing through. She was no longer the aloof, hard-headed business executive, but a woman given over to sorrow and some regret.

'If only we had come here sooner,' she said, and then

with a firmer resolution, 'I vowed I would never use these words because "if only" is such a futile way of looking back—if only we hadn't worked so hard to build up an empire; if only we had taken more time for ourselves; if only I had had Martha when I was young! They're all the chances you take. You have your own priorities in life and it's no use bemoaning the fact if things go wrong. We had a good life. Don't think I'm complaining, because I'm not. I had all I wanted in the beginning, and we had Martha, but sometimes—just sometimes—I wish . . .'

'What will you do now?' Anna asked after a moment.

'I'm not sure. I haven't been able to think straight these past few days since it happened. I need time, but I think I will probably go to Switzerland in the end. You see, Martha's future was so important to us. We had it all planned. She would go to school there and learn about independence. I don't think that has changed.'

'Andreas is worried about you,' Anna said.

'I know. He has been a dear friend and we will miss him tremendously.'

'But—you will see him in Switzerland.'

'On and off. We have been friends for over four years, Anna, more like brother and sister if not quite mother and son!' A faint smile touched Lara's pale lips. 'Andreas will go a long way in his career. He has always been ambitious and he will succeed.'

'Not without you, surely.'

'Oh, we won't part company, if that's what you mean.' Lara's eyes were suddenly clear as she looked back at her. 'I'll always be available to give him advice, but I think he will go ahead on his own. Philip and I taught him all we knew because we believed in him in the first place, and we'll still be partners in the hotel chain, of course. I must have someone I can rely on, you see, now that Philip isn't here. I don't think—anyone would object to that.'

'No. How could they?'

Was it possible to feel completely numbed by the truth, Anna wondered; was it possible to readjust your thoughts to a future that was not so dark?

Over tea they spoke about Switzerland, where Martha would go to school. 'It was what Philip wanted,' Lara said. 'Yes, I think I have finally made up my mind to live there in the future.'

'Will you sell the villa at Pedhoulas?' Anna asked.

'Yes.' Lara's decision was immediate. 'I have no more use for it and I couldn't live there alone. If I want to come to Cyprus I can have this suite, but I'm sure Switzerland will satisfy all my future needs. Perhaps one day you will come and visit me.'

'I'd like to do that very much,' Anna said without hesitation.

When she rose to go Lara walked to the lift with her. 'Thank you for coming,' she said. 'I will always be grateful to you, Anna.'

CHAPTER EIGHT

THE next few weeks were among the busiest of the hotel year. Guests came and departed, there were festivities everywhere, and at the beginning of June an area of excavation was opened up along the boundary of Candy's Place and the Villa Severus. A small colony of students came to work on the dig, revealing the foundations of a substantial residence and several smaller houses where some pottery was found but very little else.

By the middle of the month the temperature had soared into the nineties and even the wind blowing in across the bay was hot.

At the end of June Dorothy Rossides and John Malecos announced their intention to marry. It came as no surprise to Anna, who could not grudge her mother this second chance of happiness, although she knew that it would leave a gap in her own life which would be difficult to fill. Dorothy remained at the estate house till a week before the wedding, returning to the coast because she was determined to be married from her own home.

It was to be a quiet affair because neither of them were young romantics, but Anna knew that half of Limassol would want to be at the church of St Barnabas that Sunday afternoon to wish her mother well. John, too, had many friends of long standing, and Lara and Martha would also be there. They still occupied the private suite at the Crescent Beach, although Lara was already making her preparations to go to Switzerland in September.

Andreas, who had been as busy as Anna during these intervening weeks, was determined to arrange a reception for the newly-weds at the Crescent Beach.

'I want to make it really special,' he said to Anna. 'Something they won't forget.'

On the wedding morning he came to the villa to take them to church, looking heartbreakingly handsome in his formal suit, and Dorothy greeted him with a special smile. She looked radiant in her simple grey chiffon dress with a wide-brimmed hat to match and holding the small spray of apricot-coloured roses Anna had bought for her.

'We're ready to go,' she said, taking his arm as they went out to his car. They were a family again.

Anna, in attendance, wore a deep apricot-coloured dress, and Lara appeared at the church in elegant black with Martha in white walking sedately by her side. There was no sign of Susan, but Helena and Kypros Masistas occupied a prominent pew near the front, smiling benevolently at everyone within radius. It was several minutes before Anna saw Nikos sitting several pews behind his parents. He was squiring Susan, in shocking pink, who had evidently made a conquest and wanted everyone to acknowledge the fact. Anna realised that she had neither seen nor heard from Nikos since that fatal afternoon at Khrysokhou Bay so that, too, was the ending of a chapter.

After the nuptials they gathered in the sun outside the church, effectively blocking the roadway for several minutes as they left the pavement to greet one another and renew old acquaintances, holding up the traffic on every side because they were too happy to care.

Nobody seemed in a hurry to rush away, but at last Andreas decided it was time to go. He touched Anna on the arm.

'It's getting late,' he said, 'and Mama is beginning to look tired.' He had given her mother away at Dorothy's request and Anna could only think of him as he had walked down the aisle with her mother on his arm coming straight towards her where she waited at the altar rail.

'How are we going back?' she asked.

Suddenly he laughed. 'Martha has insisted on accompanying the bride!' he said, 'so it looks as if you'll have to come with me. I'll pick up Lara if I can find her,' he added, 'but there are plenty of cars to cope with everybody.'

They drove back to the Crescent Beach alone, a short interlude in a busy day which left Anna strangely moved.

'Thank you for all you've done, Andreas,' she said as they covered the short distance along the broad coastal road to the Crescent Beach. 'I appreciate it very much.'

He smiled at her acknowledgement, turning the car into the entrance of the hotel where a white-suited porter sprang to open the door for her.

The reception had been planned in the large dining-room which looked like a bower of flowers. Andrea had spared no expense and she noticed that the pink roses on the tables were exactly the same apricot shade as the posy she had chosen for her mother. He had thought of every detail—or somebody had!

Dorothy was obviously touched by his gesture. 'If I had really been his mother,' she said wistfully, 'he couldn't have given me a happier send-off.'

It was all over far too soon. The cake was cut, the favours distributed and the toasts duly drunk, and after all that Dorothy did look tired.

'We're not going very far,' John assured Anna, taking her aside to say goodbye. 'Just to the mountains for a day or so till I have some adjustments done to the flat. Then, later on, we may go to Rome.'

When the last of their guests had gone Anna walked back to the Villa Severus alone, aware of the sudden emptiness in her heart as she walked through the deserted hall on to the loggia overlooking the bay. Most of the residents were at dinner or still in the bar behind the trellised screen, and the loggia itself was deserted.

She stood there for a moment, listening to the sea before she moved towards the terrace edge to look along the shore where the lights of Candy's Place glittered against the velvet darkness of the sky.

'Are you missing her already?'

She knew that Andreas was standing close behind her although she had not heard him cross the terrace to her side.

'I feel—alone,' she admitted into the quiet night. 'I have never felt like this before.'

He put his hands on her shoulders, turning her to face him. 'You needn't feel alone, Anna,' he said. 'Never again. Surely you know that I love you and I need you to love me in return. I've always felt that this would happen—that Mama would marry again some day and we would come together in the end. I've waited and hoped for it for a long time.' He moved suddenly, taking her fully into his arms. 'Say you love me! I want to hear you say that more than anything else in the world because I've loved you always—all through those precious years when we were growing up here together. That's why I wanted the villa as it was—as the only real home I had ever known. I wanted us to be here together, always.'

She looked up at him in the gathering dusk. 'I love you,' she said without hesitation. 'I have loved you from the beginning, for as long as I can remember, but when I thought you had—deserted us I had to hate you, but all the time I must have known it was love.'

He kissed her then with a passion she had not expected in him, holding her close against his heart.

'I must have known you could never have married Nikos,' he said. 'You were always mine. Nikos—no one could ever have loved you like this.'

'I thought I had lost you for ever,' she murmured. 'I thought Lara——'

He held her away from him, laughing gently. 'Lara?' he said. 'How could you ever think we were in love? She was my friend and sponsor, just as Philip was. We were a unit—something more than friends.' He gazed out across the bay. 'That's what made it so difficult to take when he died so suddenly,' he admitted roughly. 'Lara will come back here from time to time,' he added quietly, 'and we'll be neighbours as well as partners because one day I hope you and I can turn this place back into a home again where we can bring up a family of our own.' He looked up at the loggia where the shadows of the arches lay darkly on the marble paving stones, 'That's what I wanted when I first came back to the island,' he confessed. 'I never thought of our old home as an hotel—never wanted it to be one.'

'It will all be the same again,' Anna said, her eyes shining with happy tears. 'Just as it always was, Andreas—just as you planned.'

They turned away from the sea back along the loggia into the friendly warmth of the hall where the lights burned steadily, welcoming them into a future that was suddenly bright with love.

Can you keep a secret?

You can keep this one plus 4 free novels

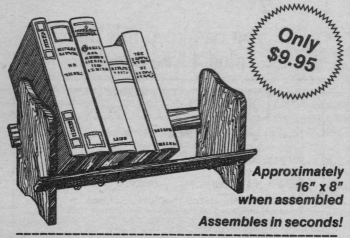